YEAR TWO

2020

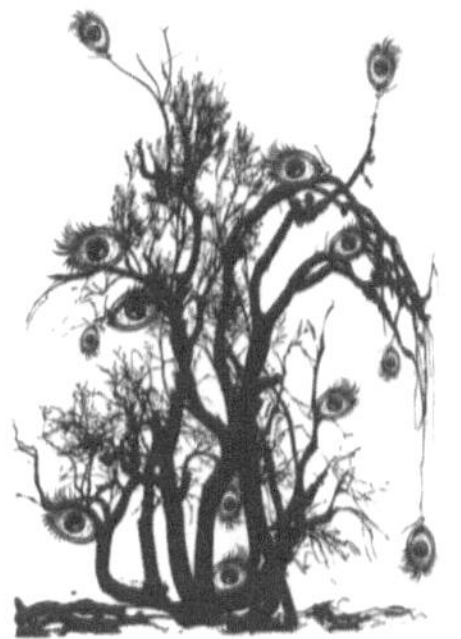

Compiled & Edited by
Ben Thomas & D Kershaw

Also available from Black Hare Press

DARK DRABBLES ANTHOLOGIES

WORLDS
ANGELS
MONSTERS
BEYOND
UNRAVEL
APOCALYPSE
LOVE
HATE
OCEANS
ANCIENTS
666

BHP WRITERS' GROUP SPECIAL EDITIONS

STORMING AREA 51
EERIE CHRISTMAS
BAD ROMANCE
TWENTY TWENTY
SCHOOL'S IN
JIBBERNOCKY

OTHER VOLUMES

DEEP SPACE
WHAT IF?
KEY TO THE KINGDOM
BEYOND THE REALM
DEEP SEA
BANNED
WETWARE

SEVEN DEADLY SINS

PRIDE
LUST
SLOTH
ENVY
GREED
GLUTTONY
WRATH

ANNUALS

YEAR ONE
YEAR TWO

THIRTEENS

PASSENGER 13
QUIETUS 13
ZER HOUR 2113
13 DROPS OF BLOOD
13 VICTIMS

Twitter: @BlackHarePress
Facebook: BlackHarePress
Website: www.BlackHarePress.com

"I have finished another year," said God,
"In grey, green, white, and brown;
I have strewn the leaf upon the sod,
Sealed up the worm within the clod,
And let the last sun down."

"And what's the good of it?" I said.
"What reasons made you call
From formless void this earth we tread,
When nine-and-ninety can be read
Why nought should be at all?

"Yea, Sire; why shaped you us, 'who in
This tabernacle groan' -
If ever a joy be found herein,
Such joy no man had wished to win
If he had never known!"

Then he: "My labours - logicless -
You may explain; not I:
Sense-sealed I have wrought, without a guess
That I evolved a Consciousness
To ask for reasons why.

"Strange that ephemeral creatures who
By my own ordering are,
Should see the shortness of my view,
Use ethic tests I never knew,
Or made provision for!"

He sank to raptness as of yore,
And opening New Year's Day
Wove it by rote as theretofore,
And went on working evermore
In his unweeting way.

New Year's Eve **by Thomas Hardy, 1906**

Table of Contents

BLACK HARE PRESS

YEAR TWO

Foreword

We set off at the beginning of 2020 full of new resolutions, big plans, a spring in our steps, and a new-year-new-start attitude…only to find ourselves bang in the middle of a global historical event. For many of us, the adjustment has been hard—dealing with isolation, mental health issues, personal problems—but we think there's finally a light at the end of the tunnel. We're hopeful for a notably different 2021, incorporating all the good bits (yes, there were some!) of 2020.

But, even in all the madness that's been going on, we saw some positive gains. We're thankful for all the new readers who took advantage of being at home and bought and enjoyed our publications.

As always, we're still learning every day—opening themes, trying new internal styles, finessing—and we hope to keep doing that through next year. Hopefully, you'll stick with us for more fiction fun in 2021.

Love and kisses
Ben & Dean

Black Hare Press

YEAR TWO

DARK MOMENTS

BLACK HARE PRESS

Thanks, Pop Culture

by Neen Cohen

"You gunna sparkle in the sunlight?" She laughs, and I smile as we waltz back to her place.

Pop culture had made hunting so much easier. And a lot more fun.

"May I?"

"Oh, of course." She giggles, believing the act. "Come on in."

I step in and watch her as she reveals her flesh.

Her smile slips; from eyes, and then lips. Horror freezes her as she takes in the twisted veins of my body.

I lick her skin, sending poison to freeze her permanently.

Her eyes her only means of communication. I bask in the fear for days.

Beware the Plastic Teeth

by D.J. Elton

Brian sighed. *Halloween props for tonight. Ridiculous.*

Mum was keen. "Here's twenty. Take your sister."

Brian scowled. Jodie pulled his arm, squirming and squealing.

Witches, vampires...rubbish! Brian screened the shop, unimpressed. Jodie found a packet of fangs. *Gold!*

"Ha! Made in China." Brian grabbed it, slipping a pair in his mouth.

"Rarrrrrrrhhhh!" He roared at Jodie, who screamed and hid.

"Can I help?" A delicate woman appeared. Brian gulped. She was beautiful. He tried to remove the fangs, but they stuck in his mouth. Old memories emerged.

She smiled as Brian lunged forward. A kiss was all it took.

Hard Wood

by Hari Navarro

The tip of his stake pushes the cloth from my chest and settles against my hardening nipple. I prick my tongue on the rapier prongs in my mouth, and I open the moist stick of my lips and offer he, who would be my killer, a glimpse of their reddening shine.

"I'm human. See in me a ghost of the life that was torn from my neck?" I whisper as my long fingers wrap around the hard black wood in his fist.

"I see you. I'm not here to kill the beast. I'm killing the wretched man you once were."

Liquid Diet

by Steven Holding

Fluids feed us, true enough, but not all rely upon the claret for sustenance.

Divergent breeds born with differing needs; consequently, some thirst for more…eclectic refreshment. The Lachrymose relish the taste of tears, breaking a heart or an arm before a feast. A Perspiration Prince favours the flavours of an athlete's fresh armpit, whereas some poor suckers simply sup upon the seed of a man.

Myself?

All that is required is one fleeting glimpse of my true countenance. The sight of such delights and everyone soon feels the lukewarm tickling trickle of fear.

It's a piece of piss, really.

The Cautious Predator

by G. Allen Wilbanks

These children have no appreciation for the subtlety of the old ways. They flaunt what they are for the whole world to see, confident in their invulnerability.

Books and movies make them bold. Humans love vampires for the moment. Revere them. Want to be them. But that will change. It always does.

Eventually, the fear will outgrow the worship as the humans realize the true risk they face from us. They will turn on us. The careless will be weeded out. It is only a matter of time.

And for the cautious predator, like myself, there is nothing but time.

The Power of Love

by Paula R.C. Readman

"The first bite is as powerful as love," he whispered. Cold lips brushed mine as his stale breath caressed my neck. In his empty eyes, death lingered.

His chilling arms snaked around my waist, leaching my body's heat.

I shivered.

The moonlight edged his fangs as he bent to take a bite. I tried not to stare at his bloodless lips as I gently manoeuvred the stake into my hand.

"No, love's full of warmth and passion," I said driving the stake upwards.

After I brushed the dust from my clothes, I crossed his name off my list and left.

Moonlight

by Annie Percik

I am a light in the darkness, obscured by the shadows of the world. You are drawn to me by fascination and longing. You seek my brightness, shining amidst the dullness your mundane life. Witness my full unshielded splendour and you will be consumed, dying in ecstasy to feed my light. This is an experience that cannot be transcended. Fitting then that it should be your last. Your essence subsumed but living on forever. Release your memories, your loves, your pain. The stolen experiences that give my existence reflected meaning. Give up your life so that mine will never end.

The Day I Died

by Clint Foster

There was no warning before I died.

A sharp flash of pain, a weakness as the blood left my body, then I was tired, and I slept. I can't say how long I rested, nor could I have guessed where I was. I remember the taste of metal and the fire in my throat and gut as I was fed. When I woke, I wondered if this was heaven, or perhaps hell. Maybe it was both, or neither, or something in between. Yet I woke, and I woke hungry, and where most newborns mewl for milk, I craved only blood.

The First Bite

by Jodi Jensen

Lush, full, delicious lips were all he could think about. All he could focus on when she was near.

And man, she was near.

So close he could smell her coconut shampoo. See the vein throbbing in her neck as she gazed at him, breathless.

He wrapped an arm around her waist and swept her against his body. "I'm going to eat you up."

"Promise?" she whispered, a seductive smile curving her ruby red lips.

"I promise." He dipped his head closer. "And I always keep my promises."

He bit her lip, savoring her gasp, her blood, then her screams.

Carnival Nights

by Trisha Ridinger McKee

Patsy was plain and blended in well at the carnivals. No one noticed if she had been at the previous town. No one thought to mention her when the authorities asked questions. She slipped in and slipped out with that plain face and those hungry eyes. The same eyes that looked away right before sweeping in for a bite. She did not enjoy the terror she evoked from the man lured behind the cotton candy stand or the young teenage boy that took her to the field for the fireworks. There was only hunger nipping where her soul had been.

Countess D

by Robin Braid

"The Countess must die," the cry went up as the crowd surged forward, "Destroy the demon."

The flames held aloft illuminated the tree lined roadside. Creatures of the night blinked once in the glow then scurried for sanctuary. I walked among the throng of townsfolk, head hooded and bowed. They did not, could not, know my true heart.

The castle would burn that night. But come sunrise I would be gone and you would be within me, always.

I touched my neck, fingertips traced the marks there. This was your final hour, my love, but it was my new dawn.

Camponotus Vampiricus

by Robert Bagnall

Doug sharpens Swan Vestas. Making both ends useful, he says. "Wait until dark. Then you'll see."

We watch purple dusk turn to night through the broken sash window.

A rattle at first, then a scratch. Doug's flashlight scans the floor.

"Becky!"

Doug's lit match waves a tide of them back. I swing my miniature spear, stick it to the critter through the thorax. It writhes. *Becky Parsons, vampire killer!*

Suddenly something's not right. "Doug?"

By my ankles, the flashlight is carried away, turned on us. Doug's slumped, bitten, jerking. I'm down to my last match. The vampire ants have won.

Razor

by Rich Rurshell

I could see it in his eyes. He knew what was about to happen. It was a look of both fear and resignation. He truly loved me, I now know that for sure. He had accepted me for who I am, despite what I am. Even that never seemed to worry him…until he cut himself whilst shaving this morning.

As I entered the bathroom, he turned to me, that haunted look on his face.

"Elizabeth?"

I saw the blood running down his throat and I lost control. A frenzy. I left him lifeless. Empty.

Those eyes will forever haunt me.

Last Call

by Stephanie Scissom

Jackson called at 9:57 a.m. Still sulking from last night's argument, Freya almost didn't answer.

"Babe!" he gasped. "Something bad's happened. A plane hit my building. There's a fire and I might not—I love you, Freya."

The line went dead. She ran to the television and screamed as she watched the south tower fall.

Why hadn't she turned him? He'd begged her. Now he was gone.

Her centuries weighed upon her. Devastation. Grief. She was done with this evil world.

If Jackson was burning, she'd burn, too.

Freya stepped into the September sun. Her skin began to smoke.

Regrets

by Steven Lord

The yearning starts off in the morning as a low buzz, just beyond the limits of hearing. The shadow of an itch, not yet demanding your full attention.

By midday, it's harder to focus. Your mind starts to wander down dark, familiar paths.

By sundown, it's a full-throated roar. Everything you do, see, hear, warped by that single desire. Your mental protestations crumble in the face of the onslaught.

That night—every night—hot blood will mingle with hot tears of shame.

This is not what you wanted. But this is what you have. For now and eternity.

Courage

by Catherine Kenwell

It had been too long. The infernal thirst after the apocalypse had depleted her. There was nothing left.

First, she feasted on the recently deceased; she was fortunate to find bodies, still warm after the blast. But their blood was sick, tainted with poison. It made her feel ill, a malaise she hadn't felt in hundreds of years.

Could she find the courage and strength?

Was she pure enough of spirit?

She caressed the white oak stake, tracing its length with her long fingers. No more daylight. No lethal sun. No easy way out.

She positioned its tip, and plunged.

Winter Kiss

by Donald Jacob Uitvlugt

Nothing is more beautiful than blood on new-fallen snow.

Lilith scents the air. Her prey's blood calls to her. Even without the footprints, she could find him anywhere in the forest. Anywhere in the world.

He fires his weapon when he sees her. The exquisite pain is a mere inconvenience. She swoops in and breaks the gun. Then she takes the back of his neck.

His urine-soaked pants steam in the cold.

"All I want is one kiss…"

He lets her—they always do.

After the kiss, she drops his body and smiles. Face pale. Lips red.

Blood on snow.

Only When I Sleep

by J.W. Garrett

Shana glanced upward. Bits of darkened sky lightened; daybreak wouldn't be far behind. Her coffin's comfort wasn't far. She'd easily make it.

But more than anything, Shana wanted to be a creature of the light. Instead, she lurked in gloom, syphoning from her prey, never to experience the radiance she yearned for deep inside. When she slept, colours of the sun warmed her, seeping through her blackness even though she was shut in tight.

Reaching toward the brightness she craved, Shana waited…

Her blood pulsed as the brilliance took her, and in a burst of flame, she met the dawn.

The Party

by Pavi Raman

The Dardanellis threw the best Halloween parties in the neighbourhood. They were a charming couple, old school. So of course there were rumours. Everything from unholy rituals to BDSM.

The theme: vampires. Perfect with Paulo's overbite and Sophia's pale skin.

Paulo opened the door. Eerie silence filled the house.

"Party downstairs. The basement is soundproofed," he explained, grinning.

"Kinky."

"You have no idea."

"Oh, but I do."

We both laughed.

I seized him, tore his neck with my fangs.

The body tumbled down the stairs, and Sophia screamed.

I locked the basement door behind me.

This party was just beginning.

Embrace

by Maura Yzmore

How long has it been? A century or two? Thanks to me, you're not the worse for wear, yet my gift has always offended you.

I wonder why you asked to meet here, the place where you briefly loved me, where you said you wanted to be with me forever, then abandoned me with hatred and disgust after I'd made your wish possible.

My heart leaps as you embrace me.

Your arms fold behind my back. I feel you swiftly pull something out of your sleeve.

My head spins with the joy of your touch, the stake piercing me through.

Gift Wrapping

by Glenn R. Wilson

"We've gathered here to celebrate the ascension of our newest member," says the headmaster while pointing at me. "Bring in the reward."

Within moments a cart appears in front of me. Upon it, something squirms within a canvas bag sealed with rope tied in a bow. I reach out and open the card attached to it.

"Congratulations!" it says.

A smile graces my lips as I hurriedly expose its contents.

The sound of applause drowns out the screams of the young girl as my teeth press deeply into her throat. I watch her eyes close as I get my fill.

Weak Timid Afraid

by Kathy Slater Neilsen

Her skin translucent, veins within, a road map to her heart. The heart I've been cast from. I loom over her, wood stake poised.

Eyes open, burning, upon me.

"Get off." She flicks me aside, a broken, pathetic mortal.

"Turn me" I plead. "If you love me, turn me."

"Love? You're weak, timid, afraid. Turning won't change that." She stares. Laughing. "You're good for one thing only."

She's upon me, wild, fierce, hungry. Cold fangs pierce warm flesh. An oaken stake intervenes. Startled, eyes wide, her heart stutters, stops. Eyes dim. Blood gushes. I drink.

I am…

Immortal.

Vampire.

A Shot of Carmilla

by Joachim Heijndermans

Funny, a thing like her being so beautiful. Asleep, she could pass for human, were it not for the teeth at the corners from her mouth. Sleeping beauty in a drop pod.

The colony is right below us. Blissfully unaware of what is about to come down on them. Bloodsucker outbreak, brought to them by a shot of Carmilla.

Horrible way to die. And any infected survivors would get the thirst and the sun's burn, I tell you what. I'd feel bad, but one look at the poster of the King massacre kills any of that.

Green light. Bombs away.

Covert Operation Helsing: Malawi Mission

by Jacob Bowers

"You may have done your research, but you don't know a thing about this place," said my driver as we bumped along the muddy road.

I clutched my crucifix and my badge; United Nations Peacekeeping, Vatican Dispatch. On paper, they knew the vampire killings were third world hysteria. But in reality…they sent me.

I was scared shitless.

We stopped at the little hovel with no windows.

I entered, brandishing my crucifix in the dark before me.

I couldn't see it—only those green eyes, waiting, beckoning for me to come closer. I reached for my vial of holy water.

The Fliers Club

by James Lipson

"Are you kidding me?"

"I might be. Why?"

"Seriously? Look in the mirror, tell me what you see."

"I see a well-appointed Armani suit, impeccable Testoni Oxford shoes, one of twelve Rolex Zerographe Reference watches and a pair of Bvlgari BV 106K glasses."

"Really? Is that all you see?"

"Dimitry, I'm sure I don't know what you speak of."

"You do realize your fang implants aren't invisible, yes?"

"I thought they gave me an air of terror."

"Vladimir, while impeccably dressed, an aging vampire with dentures does not invoke the level of fear or terror our membership requires. Application denied."

The Kiss

by Michael Crow

The bite wasn't what I expected. A gentle wispy kiss just below the beard line, whispering honey-laced allurements in my ear. Languor took hold of me and warmth filled my body and before long I passed into darkness. It wasn't the terror and pain that stories tell but gentleness and quittance.

There was plenty of scalding, piercing pain like being impaled by a thousand searing pikes. The pain came when I awoke from death. After pain came gelidity and nihility, a void in my being. A gnawing urge deep within to fill the void. A hunger for succulent satisfying blood.

Next Time, Take the Stairs

by Nicole Little

My new job has phenomenal perks: travel, luxury accommodations; no expense spared. So the booking at this creaky old London hotel surprises me, I'll admit.

Late for a meeting, I hop on the empty elevator; impatiently check my watch as the slow descent halts several floors down. The group waiting there shuffle their feet, glance at me awkwardly, but no one makes a move to get on. As the doors whisper shut, I hear a woman mutter something that chills me to my core:

"Why are there so many people on that bloody lift?"

But…I'm alone.

Aren't I?

Blame it on El Trauco

by Ximena Escobar

Knowing the fate befalling virgins in the forest, Mirén never sent her daughter for firewood. Therefore, her husband's claim that she'd been taken *by El Trauco*, met her suspicion.

Although the ugly dwarf was to blame for every fatherless child in Chiloé, something about her daughter's eyes told of a far uglier monster. *El Trauco's* victims slept unaware through his attacks, but her daughter hadn't since held her mother's gaze and couldn't lose a painful frown.

When the child was born, bearing a hideous singular eyebrow like her husband's, Mirén gripped his axe, splitting his head—and monobrow—in two.

Sausage Soup

by Jacob Baugher

When the three sweating golfers in Speedos sink into the hotel's Jacuzzi, I float to the pantry. Chef Jimmy never notices me. He's too old to believe in ghosts. I grab onions, carrots, and the butcher knife too.

When I return, I add the veggies, some spices, crank up the heat. Conversations cease. They drift off to sleep.

I slit their throats, crack their heads. The sluggy, grey ramen slops into the bloody bubbles. I follow, nibble at their bones.

The stained Speedos float to the surface. Housekeeping will clean up later. For now, I slurp my noodly sausage soup.

Night Drive

by R.J. Meldrum

He woke, disturbed. The dream had been vivid, violent. Their car had crashed; metal, glass and flesh, all ripped apart. His mood changed when he saw everything was the same. The same road, the same darkness. His wife was still driving, staring out the windshield into the night.

"I just had the strangest dream."

She didn't answer.

"I dreamt we crashed. That we died."

She turned to look at him. The front of her face was a bloodied mess, her eyes missing. Blood oozed out of her wounds. She grinned with a toothless mouth.

"That was no dream, my love."

I Can't Stand the Rain

by Frances Tate

"And the dreams?" the psychiatrist asks.

"Stopped," I lie, won't admit the rain still brings them on. Worse than ever.

I drive home, wipers dancing.

Cooking makes me feel better; a romantic meal for one. Italian. Plenty of wine. I go to bed feeling relaxed.

Dream.

I wake, soaked and shivering.

In my dream, a monster entered a random family's home. Tore the children apart first.

Shredded Mum as she tried to reach them. Took a bullet, didn't stop. Ripped Daddy asunder.

Rising, whimpering and sore, I see the blood-streaked monster at the bare first-floor window: Scream.

At my reflection.

Lady in White

by Harry J. Canis

"Headless horse-riding monk! Really?"

Harry gazed into the flames "It's true! And then there's the Lady in White story."

The group of teenagers looked uneasily at each other. The Abbey ruins were spooky enough at night, without ghost stories.

"She promised her only love that she'd walk this trail every day until he returned from a voyage. He never did. Legend says she still walks here, waiting. Anyone who blocks her path dies."

"The path we are sitting on?"

Harry grinned "Yep!"

Police found all but one of the missing group, dead beside a burnt-out fire, seawater in their lungs.

Once

by Raven Corinn Carluk

Maggie stirred the stew, staring vacantly at it. Daddy would be home soon, would expect dinner to be hot and beer open and on the table. She didn't want another spanking; her behind still had welts from the last time.

Daddy stomped in through the back door. "Smells just like your momma's cooking."

You look like your momma. You taste like your momma.

Maggie had learned a lot from Momma. Cooking. Cleaning. When enough was enough. Where to forage in the woods. What could be eaten or not.

Momma had always said all mushrooms could be eaten. Some only once.

The Shape of Darkness

by K.B. Elijah

At first, I thought it was the real estate agent. Who else bothered to come onto the property but Sandy White, her box of cheap biscuits in one hand and annual lease documents in the other?

But Sandy was pink cardigans and curls, not this hunched figure that loomed in the shadows of the moonlit driveway. Why did the shape of its head angle so? Was it just a trick of the darkness that lent it a gaping hole instead of a mouth?

I switched on the headlights, preparing to laugh at myself.

But the thing was wearing my face.

You Came to Me

by Paula R.C. Readman

In the depth of a cloudless night, you came to me. Your cheeks all aglow and lips slightly parted.

"A Whiter Shade of Pale" tunelessly ran through my head. I reached for your hands. Cold to the touch, I cared not.

"Come. Lay beside me, my darling, for I shall warm you up."

Wordlessly, you climbed in. I ignored the odour of decay that perfumed your skin and the worms and dirt that fell from your hair.

As the moonlight shone off my gravestone, I wrapped the shroud around us; glad to have you finally back in my arms again.

Family Reunion

by Joel R. Hunt

The months after she died felt like a thousand lifetimes, and each one was unbearable without her. When she appeared at the foot of my bed, I knew she had returned to release me from my torment. Her eyes glowed. Her face shone. Her finger beckoned.

God, how I missed her.

"Join me," she sang.

"Yes, my love," I answered. I rose, grabbed the nearby razor and snapped it in two. She smiled as my trembling fingers took the blade.

"We'll be a family again," I whispered.

I pushed open the door. Walked over to the nightlight.

"All of us."

Bogeyman

by Andreas Hort

"Mm, Liam," purred the raspy voice. "You look so delicious…"

"Daddyyy!"

Thunderous footsteps. Dad barged into the room.

"What's going on? Liam?"

"Bogeyman!"

"Again?" Sighing, Dad switched on the light. "Where do you want me to look first?"

Liam wanted him to look in the closet. Empty. Under the bed? Also empty. Outside the window? Nothing.

Liam felt safer; maybe it had only been a dream after all. Dad killed the light, wished Liam goodnight, and left. Liam slid his feet under the covers and closed his eyes.

"So delicious…" Muffled. Under the covers.

Sharp teeth sank into his belly.

An Honest Review

by Galina Trefil

Centuries ago, he'd killed her.

She hadn't let it go. Skulking in the back during her book signing, he flipped through the hard copy whose glossy cover was a sensationalized rendition of his medieval portrait.

Many smear campaigns had been launched against him over time, but he wouldn't abide one from her, regardless of whether she knew why she was so drawn to hate him.

In the parking lot afterwards, he malingered near her car. "What do you want?" She demanded.

"An honest review," he replied, exposing her throat for the upcoming feast.

Centuries from now, would she write again?

Exterminate

by Evan Baughfman

They returned with a vengeance, with a hive mind sharing a singular goal: the eradication of the human race.

They came back bigger than before. Meaner. Angrier.

They had every right to be furious with us, of course.

We'd let them all die. Ignored scientists' warnings for decades. Caused the creatures' untimely demise with habitat loss and pesticides.

Now, their swarms were massive and many. They attacked with two-inch-long, mutant stingers. Their venom rotted our brains. Turned us into bloodthirsty, mindless cannibals.

They'd found a way to exterminate us.

Unfortunately, we couldn't figure out how to exterminate them.

The zombees.

One

by Chris Bannor

For three days my brother and I ran. We screamed, pushed and pulled, and fought until we were free. We were both drained, and the house had seemed safe enough. Distant enough.

They crept in while we slept.

My brother opened his eyes moments after me and I could see the fear. He heard them too. There was no escape this time.

"The gun has two bullets," he whispered. I'd lied. There was one.

He was too soft-hearted to pull the trigger anyway, so he never knew. I was the only one left alive when the zombies began to feast.

This Is Where It Ends

by Wondra Vanian

Everyone knows where it started. This is where it ends.

Seven people are gathered around the fire in a draughty old cabin. They don't look it, but they're all that's left of humanity.

For the next twelve and a half minutes.

That's how long it will take the shuffling horde to trudge through the snow. After that…

The survivors aren't fighters; haven't even *seen* a zombie since before little Xander was born. They believe they're safe.

For another nine minutes and twelve seconds, they are. They'll enjoy the last minutes of Xander's fifth birthday celebration.

The last minutes of humanity.

Kill the Messenger

by Shawn M. Klimek

Kendra hurried back to the shelter to share the bad news. Dr. Armstrong's serum had backfired. Despite early hopeful signs, all those treated had eventually regressed. Worse, the contagion seemed to have evolved a new vector. Armstrong had seemed about to explain when he tried to bite her instead. Was it airborne now? She didn't dare wait to find out.

She banged on the shelter door. "It's Kendra! Quick! Let me in!"

"Are you alone?"

"Yes!"

"Wounded?"

"No!"

As the door latch clicked, she suddenly couldn't remember why she had come. But then the smell of flesh called her inside.

YEAR TWO

Surprise!

by Maxine Churchman

Sylvia, the bride-to-be, gasped when she saw the highlight of her hen weekend. Charlotte had done well; organising events on the small Caribbean Island to keep everyone partying. Now, at the end of their last meal, a huge pretend wedding cake was wheeled in and sat in the centre of the dance floor. Everyone watched as Sylvia threw the catch.

Laughing changed to screams as the zombie leaped from the cake; pinning her down. She smelled rotten meat as it bit into her face. The last thing she saw was the grinning face of Rob's ex-fiancé, watching from the crowd.

Obey

by Paul J. Scribbans

"Harry! You promised Dad!"

"I won't shoot, I'm just using the scope."

Charlotte glanced uneasily at her older brother. She'd learnt the hard way to obey her parents; Harry wasn't. Her mother told Charlotte to be quiet last year. She disobeyed and her mom died terribly.

In the gorge below their father was stalking a zombie; machete ready to cleave its skull.

"I reckon I could take it!"

"No, Harry!"

It was too late. The shot shattered the silence. Their father's knee exploded, and he went down screaming. The children watched in horror as the zombie devoured their incapacitated father.

The Last One Alive

by Andreas Hort

Every day they trudge around the city on their endless journey for satiation of their hunger. I can imagine their suffering; I'm starving, too. Only not for flesh. For human contact. For the last six years, day after day, I've had no one to talk to but myself. I... I think I might be the last person alive.

But there's a way to satisfy my hunger.

They always travel in packs, you know? They're never alone. So, I'm gonna head out now, to join them. I'm terrified. Of the teeth, the pain... but I'm more terrified of another day alone.

New Beginning

by Melinda Pouncey

It began with a worldwide contagion. Warning signs were ignored, governments slow to respond. It spread rapidly, overwhelming resources, crashing economies. Then, just as quickly as it started, it was gone; and most of the population with it.

They didn't die, that would have been a mercy. Instead, they lingered on, blind, pale, walking corpses shut up in their homes, afraid to come out into the light. We left them there. We were used to living rough. Now in scattered communities far from the plague ridden cities, we share, we work together.

I never knew there were so many stars.

Time and Decay

by Zoey Xolton

Rayne's heartbeat thundered in her ears until the world fell away, and there was nothing but her shuddering, panicked breath, and the steady, hypnotic rhythm of blood roaring through her veins.

Plastered against a cold concrete pylon, hidden in the shadow of the interstate bridge, a hoard ambled by just feet away. There were hundreds of rotters, maybe a thousand; all stumbling along in an endless procession of decay.

The gurgling, rasping moans unnerved her, and she unconsciously side-stepped—a plastic bottle crushing underfoot. The crunch brought the hoard to an immediate stand-still and she froze.

Her time was up.

Watch Where You Step

by Jodi Jensen

"Mom! Dad!" Kelly's shouts were met with a clattering noise from the other room. She raced toward the kitchen. "Mom? Dad? Let's go!" Her foot hit the tiled floor and she slipped, landing her on her butt. "What the he—"

Feet shuffling, her mom turned, dead grey eyes staring, jaw chomping.

Kelly scrambled backward. Her hand smacked the sticky floor, and something smashed beneath her palm with a *pop*.

Her stomach lurched as she glanced down.

An eyeball…

Her dad lay on the floor next to her, empty eye socket gaping, throat gurgling.

Fuck…

He reached for Kelly's leg.

Saviours

by Dustin Pinney

The last survivor screamed as the creatures brought him to the ground, reached through his flesh, pulled away his lean meat, snapped apart his ribcage, gripped his lungs, and dug out his final breath.

They devoured him without pleasure, leaving nothing but red and bone.

Now, the undead were without purpose. The Earth forced them from the soil to consume and cleanse its surface of the dangerous parasites threatening to destroy it. The task was completed.

The ground opened up. The saviours of Earth collapsed and were welcomed back into their final resting places.

All was as it should be.

The Unturned

by Nicole Little

Holing up in this ramshackle cabin was our first mistake, but we'd run out of options.

Now we're surrounded.

They pound on the door seeking entrance. And though they mumble amongst themselves, no words are discernible to us through the splintered wood. The children – our poor children; they cower, clutching at their mothers ragged shirttails. The stench of fear in the room is tangible.

We know this is the end.

With a thunderous crash the door gives and the mob breaks inside.

"Aim for their heads boys!" I hear them shout as they open fire.

The humans. The unturned.

Bleeding, Blending, and Ending With The Living Dead

by Steven Holding

Slow shuffle, like a senile senior citizen. Shoulder to slumped shoulder. Your own odour, Eau de decay, bothers you no longer.

You're at one with the crowd now.

Amidst this apocalypse, you experience an acceptance never found in life: not inside, doing time, nor in padded asylums.

The herd swerve, having heard a scream, moaning, closing in.

A young girl swings, smashing skulls, crushing brains. It's not enough to save her.

The pack collapses while attacking.

As she's torn in two, you catch her eye, offering a smile as you dig in.

Happy that your appetite can finally be satisfied.

Cautionary Steps

by Colleen Anderson

Sergei backed away from the greyish thing with flesh rotting off its body. It staggered toward him, moaning. "—rains."

Trembling, Sergei moved onto the muddy road, water pouring in his eyes, nearly blinding him in the darkness. If only he could reach the carriage.

"—rrrrains," the creature uttered, lifting its blackened hand and pointing.

Sergei turned, trying to climb through the carriage door when the horse, its eyes showing white, whinnied and reared at the approaching horror. As its hooves thudded into the earth, it tore away, the carriage wheels running over Sergei's body.

"Reinsss," croaked the zombie.

Celestial Game

by Abi Marie Palmer

The arrow pierced the angel's chest. Damien smirked as it plummeted towards the vast grounds of his manor. Now nobody would deny his hunting skills.

His catch plunged into the lake. Its limp husk bobbed to the surface, charred but incandescent. An exquisite specimen. When stuffed, it would look impressive in the dining hall next to the Masai lion. Now to retrieve the carcass.

The angel's eyes snapped open. It rose above the lake with a disgruntled roar and clawed the arrow from its chest.

Damien's servants found his body that night. It was displayed in the dining hall, stuffed.

BLACK HARE PRESS

The Darkness Ahead

by Brianna Witte

They came for me—pitchforks sharpened and torches glowing in the dead of night. I stood in front of my wood cabin, watching the townspeople march closer. Closer to the witch that had slaughtered their livestock and dried their crops with her dark, satanic magic. Closer to me—the evil they wanted to destroy.

They thought starvation was my intention: to kill them off slowly. Yet, destroying their food supply was just a tease. They had no idea what was lying in store for them.

Salem had come to burn a witch, but it was Salem that would burn instead.

Dunwich Desires

by Beth W. Patterson

"Looks aren't everything" is sometimes the kindest thing a person feels he or she can say. Society deemed me deformed and inbred, horrified by my colour. I often walked through thunderstorms for company.

It took that special someone to desire me, but Yog-Sothoth was not the normal lover. I thought I would savour multitudinous mouths on my flesh and the sinewy strokes of limbs reaching everywhere. Sometimes being desired means instead being turned inside out and reassembled, chewed up, digested, spat out, transformed with the power to make the Old Ones flesh.

The children are growing. The hills are alive.

Brothers

by Chris Bannor

The night rumbled its greeting as the body streaked through the atmosphere. Lightning flashed across the sky, and thunder heralded its downward descent. Few who saw it would know what it was, but to the trained eye, a fallen angel was unmistakable.

Hell would not welcome such a creature, so newly lost it still reeked of the holy.

He'd fallen years ago, over something he no longer believed. He got on his motorcycle and took to the road, headed for the other. He was no longer an angel, but he would do what he could.

Even the fallen needed brothers.

The Many Lives of Miss Creant

by Chris Hewitt

Every young witch needs the protection of a good familiar, and Tara received hers on her fifth birthday. Miss Creant, Missy for short, was the blackest of black cats, and the duo bonded immediately. Unfortunately for Missy, her ward suffered with a terrible curse that would cost Missy four of her lives, eleven whiskers, and her right eye before Tara's sixth birthday. Come Tara's seventh birthday, Missy had sacrificed all her lovely black fur, an ear, and four more lives.

When the fateful day came, Missy welcomed death. Protecting the clumsiest witch in the world had been a tough gig.

Insolence

by Jesse Highsmith

Richard's ears crackled loudly in the bubbling pot. They bobbed and swirled around the heart, fingers, and toes of the man who once shared my bed. I reserved my favourite parts of his for my necklace, though. It swung wildly between my breasts as I poured the steaming concoction over our son's corpse and yelled the ancient incantation. If anyone could bring the boy back, I felt it would be his father. Before I could finish the ritual, the cops dragged me away. The neighbours will pay for their insolence. They called me a witch, but I'm just a mother.

Water on Canvas

by James S. Austin

Standing in the newly acquired estate, a painting captured my attention. It held me in rapture.

Moving closer, my eyes drew to the galleon at its centre. The sails taut, rigging displayed in sharp lines from the strain.

My smile faded to confusion. The waves appeared rougher, spray rising off its hull.

The sea now churning in stillness. Swollen clouds above.

Phantom phosphorescent specks began dotting the blue-green strokes. A melodic hum arose in my head.

Trying to end this spiralling descent, cold salt water spilled from my mouth. Coughing. With my last moments, a great yellow eye stared back.

What He Deserves

by Heather Ewings

"I brought what you wanted."

Brown with age, the playing cards cost a small fortune and a whole weekend scouring the city's antique shops.

The witch shuffles the pack and lays three cards face up.

"You don't want to hurt him. But you want vengeance. You realise those two things are incompatible?"

"I don't want to hurt anyone. But he won't stop hurting others."

She rummages through a collection of tiny bottles and hands me one.

"Get this on his person."

"Will he suffer?"

Her gaze pierces mine, and I have to suppress a shudder.

"He'll get what he deserves."

Brew for Two

by Clint Foster

The thing about potions is, it doesn't matter who makes them or what their intention is.

A drop of jellied brain, a twist of peeled tongue, some blood flakes. You stir them all together in a cauldron—whatever brand you choose, it's not that important—and bring it to what we like to call a witch's boil. You'll know when it gets hot enough, trust me, and if you don't figure it out in time, well, it won't matter anyway. A quick stir, a tiny, tiny sip. Ahh. Brew for two.

Grab a mug, please. Me? Oh, I'm not thirsty.

Oil Slick

by Evan Baughfman

Glistening, black goo coated the surface of the penguins' pool.

Albino birds huddled, squawked on land. Though blind, the gentle giants could sense the presence of something unnatural.

I thrust a cattle prod into the "slick," zapping the dark mass, startling its many eyes open.

Tentacles formed, flailed.

Ragged mouths cried, "Tekeli-li! Tekeli-li!"

Then, silence.

I radioed other keepers. "Shoggoth escaped its tank again. Stunned it. Bring barrels for transport. Don't forget the lids."

Had to discover how the creature was getting loose!

Its jailbreaks were giving the Deep Ones needless confidence and always threw Nctosa and Nctolhu into frenzies.

Stormy Little Dream Stealer

by Hari Navarro

I felt the impact as she landed in our bed. That sickly hollow plunge common to nightmares in which we fall but never land. It was sometime after the birth of our third child, I think. And she did arrive in our bed, and she did lay waste to our passion and she turned what we had to dust.

I saw her that next day as you awoke. I saw the flurry of blackened wings as they fluttered behind the blink of your morning eyes. I saw her nesting inside you and I knew then, quite certainly, we were lost.

Fragile

by Evan Baughfman

Glass slippers sparkled on Cinderella's feet.

"They're beautiful! Perfect! Thank you!"

"Hurry along, now," urged Fairy Godmother.

"Shouldn't be late for the ball!"

Cinderella stepped towards the pumpkin carriage. The right slipper's fragile heel snapped under her weight. In fact, the entire shoe cracked.

Cinderella's foot shifted backward, slicing against broken glass. The girl fell, writhing in pain.

Her severed Achilles tendon sprayed blood.

Panicked, Fairy Godmother struggled to mend the wound with stitching spells.

Cinderella didn't dance with the Prince that night—or ever, for that matter.

She became an old maid, hobbling to the end of her days.

Needing to Forget

by David Green

"Why?" Ruby muttered to Nick.

They knelt beside the sleeping Suraz, his raven hair encrusted with filth and grease. Scabs and sores covered the Nephilim's obsidian skin.

Track marks lined his exposed arms; used needles lay scattered around him.

"We all have vices," Nick replied with a sigh.

"No," Ruby whispered, tears in her eyes. "It's like he wants to die, but he can't."

Nick grabbed a blanket and covered the fallen angel.

"He's seen perfection." Suraz's eyelids fluttered as he dreamt a drug-infused dream. "Lived there, then got cast out. Never to return. I'd do anything to forget too."

Escape

by Jacek Wilkos

I dreamed about this horrible city again. I was surrounded by monstrous structures of strange shapes and impossible angles, glowing with faint greenish light. The carvings covering them portrayed bizarre symbols and creatures. I ran through this maze of distorted reality, unable to determine directions. I felt great evil, chaos crawling from every corner.

Far off, I saw a rectangle of warm white light. I ran towards it.

I woke up. I made it; I was safe. The nightmare was over.

The darkness in the room twitched. Something else got out of the dream. It enveloped me.

There's no escape.

Protection Racket

by G. Allen Wilbanks

"Grandma, why do you put milk out at night?"

The old woman placed the shallow bowl on the windowsill and pushed the window open a few inches. "It's for the pixies, dear. When they find a bowl of milk, they know we're friendly, so they won't come inside or do us any harm."

"What kind of harm?" asked the young girl.

"Don't worry about it, dear. Run along and play."

"The girl asks a lot of questions," came a tiny voice from outside the open window.

"You got your milk, you little bastards," whispered the old woman. "Leave her alone."

BLACK HARE PRESS

The Woodsman

by Chris Bannor

They gave me an axe and sent me to cut down the heart of the forest. My path was dark; wolves snapped at my steps and gave chase as persistent as the winter snows. I took shelter in the measliest of holes and spent hours scavenging enough food to survive.

When I faltered, she found me, gave me succour and safety from harm. But it is the most bitter irony.

She has filled my heart, this heart of the forest, this girl of snow, but I am the Queen's Man.

I am the Woodsman, and my axe must be true.

Miss Scarlet Hood

by Lynne Phillips

Miss Scarlet Hood met a bad wolf in the wood.
"Where are you going dressed all in red?"
She pulled a pistol and shot him dead.
A witch appeared. "I'll cast a spell."
Miss Scarlet pushed her down a well.
An ogre grabbed at her red cloak.
A knife appeared at his fat throat.
"Got you Missy," a goblin said with a laugh.
She kicked him howling down the path.
"Don't tell me tales," her mother said,
And sent Miss Scarlet straight to bed.
"Tomorrow, I'll find a dragon that flies,
And Mother will know I don't tell a lies."

The Death of Heaven

by Lyndsey Ellis-Holloway

His wings were ablaze, the heat intense as he marched upon the Golden City, alone.

Sammael tore the Gates of Heaven from their hinges, leaving rivers of molten gold in his wake.

The Host tried to stop him, but they could not. They would not. Any who tried were devoured by flame or cut asunder by Scythe.

Entering God's Throne room, he smiled darkly. "Father, I'm home." Sammael closed his eyes, hands spread wide, his flames swirling around him.

"Son, don't!"

Too late.

A deafening explosion shook the Earth and the inferno swallowed Heaven, raining ash on the world below.

Angel, Broken

by Kelly Matsuura

"Don't touch me!" Lailah waved Reuben away.

Shame. Her emotions crackled and boiled, fighting for dominance.

Reuben, always patient, held out a wet towel. "Let me wash your wounds, Love."

Her back was bleeding afresh. Thick warm blood meeting numb skin—soaking the sheets. She no longer felt external pain.

Loss. She had fallen from Heaven to be with him. Kind, passionate Reuben. But it wasn't enough.

Regret. She didn't belong here, and she could never go back.

Anger. She clutched her dagger under the blanket. How had a mortal possessed her heart?

One sharp slice.

Now they both bled.

Enemies End

by Karen Bayly

The great witch, Ophesia, sat leaning against an ancient oak. Even though her heart was drumming its final beats, she sensed his approach.

"Come to mock my last minutes, Tarlin? I have no magic left."

The ageing wizard eased down beside her. "Even I would not hurt a dying enemy."

"Yet here you are. Why?"

"I will miss you."

Ophesia cackled heartily, then noting Tarlin's serious expression asked, "Your point being?"

"*I* still have magic."

Taking her hands, he drew her to her feet.

"Let's traverse the unknown together."

She smiled as he uttered his spell.

Into darkness, they flew.

A Thousand Days

by K.B. Elijah

Red lips in a pale face, puckered in surprise. Tendrils of auburn hair haloing her head as if she dances underwater. Blue eyes wet with the first vestiges of shock, death taking her before it fully formed.

Mortals and their deceptively ephemeral beauty.

I bend, sweeping a crow feather through the bloody entrails of the girl, watching as it glows and blackens. Satisfied, I release my fingers and the feather flies to my back, reinforcing my pitiful wings.

One more necessary sacrifice, one more feather. A thousand more days like this, and I will have enough to fly once more.

The Sound from the Moors

by Joel R. Hunt

I cannot describe the sound that emanated from the moors all those years ago, nor speculate of its cause. All I can state with certainty is that it did not belong to this world.

The sound haunted my dreams for years. At last, starved of sleep, I came to hear it even in waking, echoing through my halls.

It was a relief to be committed to Arkham Sanitorium. The asylum became my blessed, silent refuge.

Yet my respite did not last.

The doctors here have no human voice.

When their mouths open, I hear only the sound from the moors.

On Thunderous Wings

by Zoey Xolton

The eldritch gods of the ever deep stir in the darkness from eternal sleep.

The Void is silent save for a single scream, originating on Earth—a little girl's dream.

Devourers of worlds from beyond the dark sheet, soon to awaken…a hunger for flesh so sweet.

From the timeless halls of Cthulhu, the Old Ones make their way to the small blue planet within the Milky Way.

Tentacles curl and golden eyes glow, the mortals have no hope—they just do not know.

By wing, tooth, tail, and claw, humanity at last will die…

Death descends, painting a blood-stained sky.

The Devourer

by Warren Benedetto

Maslowe stood absolutely still. Warm, rancid breath caressed the back of his neck.

It had come for him.

Abholos.

The Devourer.

Mist swirled around the thing, enshrouding it like unholy vestments. It was shapeless. Formless. An undulating mass devoid of features, save for a terrible maw. Its blackened lips parted to reveal crystalline teeth, curved icicles dripping with long, elastic drops of clear ooze.

What escaped from its mouth was not sound, but the absence of sound. A silence so ageless and infinite that Maslowe felt his sanity slipping away.

"Why me?" Maslowe whispered.

"Because you exist," the Devourer said.

We Can Only Fall

by Callum Pearce

Swept down from heaven on the wind of Satan's expulsion. My crime—merely witnessing dissent. I hurtled towards this filthy rock as flames ripped through my wings. In heaven, there was no pain. Now, every newly awakened nerve screams at me constantly.

They scream too, those creatures he loves so much. They howl and struggle as my knife rips through their flesh. They don't understand my gift to them. That which I am forever denied. I return them to the painless place, free them from the misery that I must endure. His children are always rising, angels can only fall.

A Successful Exorcism

by Celestine Trinidad

Father Fernando kept on chanting prayers, ignoring the screams of the demon that possessed the boy.

"You don't know what this child is!" the demon shrieked. "Without me here to stop him, he'll—"

"I cast thee out!"

A final scream, and then, silence.

"He's gone," Father Fernando said. "Niño is safe, now."

Three days later, the Santos family was found in their home, all murdered, except for their youngest, Niño, who had gone missing.

That night, during his evening prayers, Father Fernando felt someone watching him. Waiting.

When he turned, Niño grinned at him, moonlight glinting off his knife.

Madeline

by Joshua Gessner

I see a girl, hidden behind a curtain of trees, with poisoned lips and rotten teeth. Somewhere, in the pit of her, her heart is just as rotten. I believe if you slit her open, maggots and soot would be all you'd find. There is a shadow of her before she changed, signing her soul in the big black book. Yet that is all we know, the memory of her. For now, she is claimed by the unholy. She is his servant. A witch. I feel her name upon my own lips now. It stings, like a rose's thorn. Madeline.

Author's Lament

by K.T. Tate

I just wanted a muse. Something unusual to fuel my writing. But that dusty tome with its ancient rites gave me more than that.

It was not a muse summoned there, but a *thing*. Indescribable, even to a seasoned author in its unique horror. Stars burned and died within its shifting form. Its eyeless gaze burned through me, tarnishing me from the inside as I wept. The safe illusion of reality shattered.

Now it fills my mind. Taking up space, forcing me to write its heresy. My words spreading its gospel of madness. Please, I can't stop myself, I can't…

Midnight at the Gallows

by McKenzie Richardson

The corpse swings on its rope when my fingers wrap around its wrist. Tendons and muscles fray as I sever the flesh. Cracking bones, I saw through until the hand falls into my grasp.

Before dissolving into the darkness, reeking of congealing blood, I collect slabs of fat from the murderer's torso for a candle, a hair from his head to serve as its wick. Placed in the Hand of Glory, it will grant me powers unimaginable with which to exact my revenge.

They thought to burn my kind. They are not the only ones who can play with fire.

Whitechapel Rain

by Matthew Wilson

I have had dark moments since I escaped that hospital filled with fools who didn't grasp my greatness, so I had to burn them.

I wished to run into the light, but Whitechapel only has darkness and more laughing women who do not appreciate me.

The doctors I burned? I have murdered for necessities—like clothes—borrowed a dead man's name, but still my head is filled with horrid thoughts.

But I will prove those dead doctors wrong, I will try to be human, something free and undeserving of cages.

Gentleman Jack, even if I do have frequent dark moments.

Elspeth

by Jacqueline Moran Meyer

Elspeth haunts me. At night, I hear her ankle chains scrape along the floorboards towards the bedroom I share with my new bride. She's getting closer, with her bloated body now splattering water on the rug around our bed. Last night, I took to drink in the hope of not remembering her visit. This morning my new love lay dead beside me; wet footsteps led to her side of the bed. I may have married Elspeth for her money and not defended her when accused of sorcery, but never had I suspected her of truly being a witch—until now.

A Romance in Dunwich

by V.A. Vazquez

There weren't many eligible bachelors in Dunwich, but even then, all the women stayed away from Wilbur Whateley. His beard was coarse and knotted, like the hide of a mountain goat, and he smelled like cracked eggs that'd gone off.

"Disgusting," my sister would say, turning away to avoid his stare. He had to crouch down to shuffle through the bakery door, his woollen coat dragging on the cobblestones behind him.

I never turned away; I never refused to meet his eyes. Not the ones on his face and not the ones nestled in the crevices of his hips either.

The Old Switcheroo

by Steven Holding

All it took was one look at her hook nose and Danny knew that his granny was a witch.

A familiar black cat, dark pointy hat, although her number of nipples remained firmly under wraps, despite Danny lurking on the landing at bath time, desperate to administer a dunking.

He took no risks, smashing his eggshells at breakfast, stopping her from setting sail upon the seven seas, sinking fleets using sorcery.

Granny was suitably distressed.

"Don't you love me?" she pleaded. "Warts and all?"

"Oh, Nanna!" sighed Danny.

She hugged him.

Then bunged the little bastard straight in her oven.

To Serve and Obey

by Zoey Xolton

Lucifer languished upon the immense, black throne forged of dragon glass. Slumbering by his side, Lilith's great scaled tail wrapped around the dais, her bejewelled hide wreathed in living flame.

The Fallen Angel reached out and stroked the beast. "Lilith."

She growled softly, deep in her throat, a rumble of contentment shivering through her as she dreamed. Moments later, she was transformed. Awakening at the King of Hell's feet, she stretched like a cat.

A primal hunger arose within Lucifer—the fires of the Pit dancing behind his eyes.

"How may I serve you, my Lord?" she purred, her voice husky.

Bloody Mary

by Neen Cohen

She fluttered her bright blue eyes in the lights of the nightclub, taking the drink from his over-eager hands.

"Now leave."

He turned, eyebrows knitting. Tomorrow he would wonder where all the money went with no hangover to show for it.

"You make us look bad." Teara shook her head despite her ruby red smile.

"We are bad, T. Still…looking sweet and innocent isn't our fault."

"It will catch up, one day."

"Fantastic. I can't wait for the next challenge."

She leaned forward, her cleavage bringing the next victim closer.

Her nails slit through his throat, flavouring the drink.

Two Wrongs Don't Save a Changeling

by K.B. Elijah

Cold winds borne from grey skies whipped around me, mixing strands of my green hair with my tears.

"Merle." Acquisition Officer Karea fluttered down onto the bridge beside me. "You were reported for conducting an unauthorised child transfer." Her breath caught as she followed my gaze down to the violent, swirling waters beneath us. "What have you done with her?"

"Made sure the human parents keep the changeling," I snarled. "My child *will* have a better life."

Karea choked. "We've already conducted the transfer. The baby you took was…yours."

The corner of a pink blanket disappeared beneath the frothing waves.

Where's Margaret?

by Kelly Matsuura

When Wizard Qarmel took to his death bed, I didn't want him to die alone.

"What's Margaret's address? I'll send a letter," I offered. The wizard's wife had left years earlier, but no one knew her current whereabouts.

"No need." Qarmel smiled. "She's with me, always."

"She's gone. Remember?"

"Margaret is here," he insisted.

He opened his robe. In place of skin, his entire chest had become a window of frosted glass. Light from nearby candles danced on the surface.

As did Margaret's face.

Her ghostly image rippled and weaved; a prisoner forever trapped under ice.

"See? She never left."

Flames of Betrayal

by Paula R.C. Readman

Martha fed more sticks to the fire. Soon the cauldron bubbled.

She took a deep breath and began to chant. She had to get it right.

First, she added rosemary for remembrance and lavender for love.

Would he appear before her as the old witch had promised?

As the two aromas filled the air, Martha opened her eyes.

Joseph stood there. All smiles and strong in a foggy haze.

How she wanted him, her only true love.

Through the mist another appeared. Joseph wrapped his arms around her.

To the cauldron, Martha added hemlock, cursing him until his dying day.

Satan's Butterfly

by Shawn M. Klimek

Spanning the stems of a prickly cactus, a spiderweb glittered in the morning dew like a sequined doily. When a yellow hornet—actually, a demon—descended nearby, the web's owner warily revealed itself.

"What now?" demanded the spider (also a demon).

"Just watch."

Pimples like blackberry drupelets erupted all over the hornet's body. These bulged into pustules, before mushrooming into tarry lobes, like a smoker's lungs. These swelled and mutated until the mass resembled a bloated, decomposing manatee drowned in crude oil.

"Strange," gurgled the transfigured hornet.

"Don't tell *me!* Satan said you'd become a butterfly—and you believed him?"

The Old One Breathed

by Scott Wheelock

The people blanketed the ground as numerous as grains of sand upon the ocean floor. Now it stood before them as still and vast as a mountain. The God's head rose far above their view in the gathering storm clouds, but what they saw was enough. They raised their arms as one, then fell upon their knees in utter submission to their new Lord. The high priest whose people had suffered without end over the centuries raised his arms with them and, with tears in his eyes, said the words. Awakening, the Old One breathed out, and the world died.

Redecorating Heaven

by McKenzie Richardson

Merlot-hued spatters stain white feathers as I snap the final bone, hanging my newest creation up for display. These heavenly angels have gotten soft in their home of clouds, always so trusting. That was their downfall, my advantage.

I didn't fall from Heaven—I was pushed. But I crawled my way back up.

I lick the blood from my fingers, surveying the crippled bodies that decorate greying rainclouds. I've won the war and earned my right to remake this world. It will be perfect, no matter how many wings I have to break to force it into my own image.

Torches and Pitchforks

by Raven Corinn Carluk

Gavin glowered at the townfolk gathered at the base of his tower. Their grumbles had grown in volume as they worked themselves into a frenzy against the wizard within.

Amazing that one escaped experiment could so quickly whip up a mob. It wasn't like they couldn't birth more children or rebuild houses.

Thuds sounded from the door below, shouts and cheers rising. He should have exactly enough time to utter the incantation of death and teach the peasants why they feared magic. Gavin's frown became a wicked grin as syllables of power fell from his lips, a wicked wind whistling.

Everything You Know About Witches

by Warren Benedetto

"Everything you think you know about witches is wrong," Selena sobbed. She struggled against the ropes binding her to the pole.

Father Hugo stuffed kindling under the logs at her feet. He cocked an eyebrow sceptically. "Everything?"

"Everything," Selena insisted.

"Brewing potions?"

"Wrong."

"Casting spells?"

"Wrong!"

Father Hugo lit a match.

"Shapeshifting?"

Suddenly, Selena's face elongated into a long black beak. Feathers sprouted as massive wings unfolded from her back.

Her raven form lunged, driving her beak straight through Father Hugo's face.

As Selena returned to her human shape, she wiped the blood from her mouth.

"Okay, maybe not *everything*."

The Midnight Throne

by Rowanne S. Carberry

Blood-stained lips framed by onyx hair. Her body sculpted by rubies and starlight.

The prince cannot look away.

Drawn to her by magic, they dance until the room blurs.

As midnight draws near, she leans in.

"I must leave."

Without a thought he follows, tripping as he does, before finding her at the water's edge, shining in the moonlight.

"Will you join me?"

Taking her offered hand, he trails into the water.

Her consort caught, they sit together on the midnight thrones of the underworld.

All that's found of the prince on land—a bloody shoe left on the glass stairs.

Mirror, Mirror

by S.O. Green

The mirror is cracked, and the cracks are spreading.

It started when I scratched the symbol on the glass. The one from the book. The one I couldn't get out of my head.

In every line, I see a nightmare. In every facet, I see a dream. In the centre is a keyhole. Beyond, another world.

It whispers to me in my sleep. It calls to me while I work. I taste its colours and hear its darkness and feel its gentle music on my skin.

My reward is coming.

The cracks are spreading. Now they're spreading across the walls.

Paradise Mobile Estates, 2016

by V.A. Vazquez

He sat on the secondhand couch in their mobile home, springs prodding into his lower back. Flipping the tab on another can of Bud Light, he watched the moths flutter around the trailer park. One of them, with wings the same colour as greasy pizza boxes, flew a little too close to the bug zapper and then…

Zzzzzzp!

It crumpled onto the patchy grass sprouting in front of their doorstep. As he listened to the radio next door playing *música tejana,* he flexed the broken wingstalks between his shoulder blades.

"Yeah, bud," he said, toasting the fallen moth. "Me, too."

Infinity Mirror

by Beth W. Patterson

Why is the flora on my family's land suddenly so much thicker?

The sharp cry of a baby freezes me in my tracks. If someone abandoned a child, I have to make sure that it doesn't die.

Wriggling on a bed of ferns is an infant girl. But the most unsettling thing is the birthmark on her cheek. It's identical to my own.

The figure stepping into the clearing could pass for an old photograph of my mother as a young woman.

My eyes are reflected in her dagger. Her wings unfold as she croons, "Now the cycle begins again."

Spoils

by Chris Bannor

She held the knife between her teeth, hands buried second knuckle deep into the beating heart of her prey. In the deep of the woods, no one remembered to look for her kind anymore. They were easy prey, especially when they saw her diminutive size.

She might be no taller than a human child, but she was no innocent. When the others came into her sidhe, they learned. The fae may be small, but her bite was ferocious, and her tastes were bloody.

She drank, the hot splash of copper racing over her tongue was welcome after her well-won fight.

Cold Blue

by Kelly Matsuura

Celyna examined Davenall's face with a critical artist's eye.

"Your irises are like their own universe. Do all faeries have such icy blue eyes?"

"Just the naughty ones," Davenall teased.

"How will I paint the moving colours?" she mused.

"Look deeper."

"Okay." Celyna locked her gaze on his. She tried to blink but couldn't. She tried to turn her neck, also couldn't. The swirling, entrancing pools made her dizzy. Her entire body shook.

Davenall held her tight. "A little more."

"Stop! Don't do this!" She realised too late that he was draining her creative essence.

"*Leanan sídhe.*"

An artist no more.

Poor Charlie

by Hari Navarro

I was sixteen the first time. Never sensed anything like it. Such wonder. Worlds away from the fantastical lies that curled my toes and suppressed my exasperated sighs as the father spoke down from his pulpit.

Poor Charlie, loved since he was but a ball of foundling fur. His rot grabbed me, and I sat transfixed as the faeries nipped, tugged, and gulped down the flesh from the now exposed cage of his ribs.

I called my parents—they, too, stared yet all they saw were mites and flies and maggots.

I was sixteen when I first encountered the fae.

Destroyed by Silver

by Stacey Jaine McIntosh

The cold lingered, seeping into her bones. Nobody had thought to warn her what it would mean when she took up the mantle of the Faerie Queen.

"Majesty," the centaur went down on one knee and bowed before her.

"You came," she whispered. "Did you bring it?"

"I did." He unwrapped the swaddling to reveal a tiny child. Though it looked human, it wasn't.

She reached for the silver dagger she kept at her waist. And in a flash drew the knife and plunged it downwards into the infant's chest.

The sacrifice was made.

The blood of her enemy spilt.

Spoiled Goods

by Zoey Xolton

"Please!" the girl begged. "Let me free. I'll give ye' anythin' ye' desire!"

The faery turned to face her, the macabre collection of small animal skulls, and silver trinkets that adorned her waist jingling as she moved. She squatted before the terrified girl, fingering a cruel rippled blade.

"I'm afraid ye' are it, child," she answered. "My potion will no' work without the unbroken heart of a virgin."

The girl's eyes grew wide and a relieved, almost hysterical laugh escaped her. "Then I canno' be of use to ye'!" she cried. "My da has seen to tha'!"

The faery paled.

Fairies Gotta Eat

by Stephen Herczeg

I found them at the bottom of the garden. Sparkling. Beautiful. Little winged people. They looked hungry, so I left a table covered with treats on the lawn.

Mummy and I went out. Daddy did the mowing.

As the garage door went up, Mummy started screaming.

There was the table. There were the treats.

There was Daddy.

Lying on the garage floor in a pool of blood. His face was gone. Just a staring skull. They'd gobbled it all up.

I warned him before we left. I did. I told him.

"Please don't move the treats. The fairies gotta eat."

Faerie Etiquette

by Jacqueline Moran Meyer

"Stop," I yelled, too late. My fiancé had already plopped the lavender cake in his mouth. By the time I reached him, the Faerie had disappeared. I had schooled him on Faerie etiquette *ad nauseum*. Do not accept gifts.

"Didn't you notice her pointed ears, glimmering skin?"

"Yum," he mumbled.

"Did you say thank you?" I asked, my tone grim. His answer would decide our future together.

"Yep."

Distraught, I handed back his ring and walked away.

Saying thank you to a Faerie resulted in her taking your firstborn.

I discovered my pregnancy that morning.

Where could I hide from the Faerie?

The Awakening

by Eddie D. Moore

Reed couldn't believe how small his hands were as he dug and dug. Hours passed and his fingers were bleeding when he finally emerged into the night air. He softly read aloud the name written on the granite stone before him: "Reed Gormley."

Reed felt his wings spread out as he watched others flit to and fro above his head. It appeared that the legend was true and that we all lived on in a new form after death.

A wicked smile exposed tiny sharp teeth as he took to the air and growled, "You all should've treated me better."

Hunting Fae

by Karen Bayly

She watched from the alley, green eyes burning phosphorescent. Tonight, she would snag one, imprison it. Maybe she'd free it—eventually. Most likely she would torture, then kill it.

Once, the hunting was easier; lay a trap in the forest deep, and return at her leisure. These days, she relied on stealth and dark places.

Thank the goddess, only halflings believed in faeries anymore. Her sport was so much easier. All gossamer wings and wickedness, she could wrap any purebred prey in a spell a blink of an eye.

Here's one now! Male. Intoxicated. 100% human. Her favourite kind.

Faerie Things

by Chris Hewitt

Tucked off the main thoroughfare, Faerie Things boasted an extensive range of fae ingredients for the magical connoisseur. The soft tinkle of bells announced Peri's arrival.

"Can I help?" asked the rotund proprietor.

"Do you have any Faerie wings," Peri whispered.

The shopkeeper licked his lips and locked the door. "What're you after?"

"Do you have any silver sprite?"

"As it happens, I do. Fresh in this morning." The shopkeeper grinned, rummaged behind the counter and produced two tiny iridescent wings—their bloody stumps confirmed Peri's worst fears.

"Sister!" she cried, her illusion failing as anger took over.

Nice Night for a Barbeque

by Neen Cohen

Drips of fat dropped through the barbeque grill and sent flames up into the darkening sky.

"Here you go, mate." James stepped onto the patio and handed Mike a cool beer.

"Dinner won't be long." The plate hissed as James put onion on to fry.

"I'll go tell the girls." Mike disappeared inside the house again.

James opened the Tupperware container and gripped the delicate wings between thumb and forefinger.

The fairy's scream sounded like tinkling glass windchimes as he pulled the sheer material from the body.

She sizzled as she landed on the grill beside her sisters' unrecognisable bodies.

The Most Hated Candy

by Nikki DeKeuster

They smashed them. All of them.

My love and devotion lay scattered across the sidewalk outside my cemetery.

One flutter of my Luna moth wings and the vandals transformed mid-stride into piles of candy corn, sprawling over the sidewalk.

Just like my darling pumpkins.

An hour later, the foul candy reverted to its original state, splattering my bucket with gore. I picked out a glob of eyeball and chewed.

Much tastier.

Screams serenaded the neighbourhood.

The trick-or-treaters would have an awful mess to clean up and perhaps a slight bellyache.

But, that was what they got for eating candy corn.

Execution Dock

by Simon Clarke

Three tides washed over me before you covered me in tar.

But still I see you sail by, laughing at me in my cage above the Thames.

You see my empty eye sockets, the strips of putrefying flesh, the wind jerking my bones when there is no wind.

A final resting place?

No, I'm still here, dreaming of Port-au-Prince, my woman, and my gold.

I see you sail by, and I am laughing. Voodoo promised I would live forever, and so I am.

I drip contagion into the water you all drink—my pestilence will be in your city forever.

Redbeard

by Tracy Davidson

Redbeard chose the wrong island to plunder, his ship the first to find it in decades. No sealife swam near, no bird flew over. No human walked its streets.

Redbeard's first mate was first to die, skin shredded by invisible talons. The second was turned inside out, intestines wrapping around a third's neck, squeezing until it snapped.

Another disintegrated into atoms.

Redbeard's men scattered in panic, swords raised. But blades were useless against invisible enemies.

They all fell. Until only Redbeard remained.

Unlike his men, Redbeard saw his fate. Rabid dogs feasted on his flesh.

The island vanished once more.

Price of Admission

by Michelle Brett

"Shall you give your hand or your eye?"

There was no reply. The stowaway was too fixated on the knife at his throat. His limbs pinned to the deck by the unwashed bodies.

The pirate continued, "You do want to be one of us, don't you?"

With widened eyes, the stowaway tried to squirm, only to force the blade deeper into his flesh. He begged, "No…"

A snort. The smell of whiskey. The pirate turned to the crowd.

"The eye it shall be."

Cheers erupted, drowning out the stowaway's screams. From deep inside the ship, a red hot poker emerged.

Captain's Justice

by Melinda Pouncey

Captain Harrington slept with a pistol at hand for both attackers and mutineers. He ran a tight ship, which caused certain…vexations.

One night he woke to eerie silence. The door flew open and Pete Turley, the latest recipient of the captain's justice, shambled in. Skin hung in tattered shreds from his purple-mottled body. St Elmo's fire crackled hellishly about him and his upraised sword. Keel-hauled six days prior, he had been left suspended beneath the ship to rot. And rot he had.

"Someone's sent me to fetch you, Cap'n," he slurred through broken teeth. "His name is Davy Jones."

Captain Purge's Collection of Oddities

by Kelly Matsuura

"Kanami, darlin', you'll finally be whole." Captain Purge tapped his boot on the slime-covered trunk with glee.

Kanami's head floated forward, her ratty hair brushing the trunk's exterior as she gave it a fervent sniff.

Purge shuddered. Once an enchanting princess, Kanami was now a curse to the ship. He never expected the beheaded yōkai to age rapidly without her body nearby—nor that she'd feed on the flesh of his men.

There was only one solution.

Opening the empty trunk, he shoved Kanami in and slammed the lid shut.

"Toss 'er back overboard." He was truly done collecting oddities.

The Key to Keeping a Secret

by David Green

"At last," Bode cried. "The Fountain of Youth!"

Captain Kenway nodded at his first mate, letting him step forward. They'd sailed for decades before hearing whispers of Bimini, and the fountain's location.

"Aye," Kenway said, drawing his flintlock pistol, aiming at the back of Bode's head. "Everlasting life. A secret I won't share with anyone."

The blast echoed through the caves.

Stooping, Kenway cupped his hands and drank from the Fountain of Youth.

The lined, tanned skin on his hands melted as his blood burned, turning Kenway's bones to ash.

Dust swirled in the air where the Captain once stood.

The Greatest Treasure

by Nerisha Kemraj

John Smith's greedy eyes beheld the moss-covered chest.

There it lay before him.

A lifetime of searching, and endless, near-death battles brought down to this single moment.

Word of King Ragnar's lost treasure had travelled the world for centuries, and now here it was, his to own.

"I am now the richest pirate in the world!" he said, opening the chest to reveal his treasure.

But there was no gold.

No title deeds.

Jars of embalmed hearts filled the chest.

Here holds the greatest treasure anyone could ever own: that of my family.

The pirate's haggard face twisted in rage.

Jonah

by Patrick Winters

They'd plucked him from the sea one evening, lashed to a barrel and floating along, unconscious. Once he'd stirred, he gave his name as Jonah, of all things. The men wanted to cast him back to the waves that instant; the captain ignored their superstitions.

The ailment swept over them soon after, swift and horrendous, claiming them amidst their screams and choked prayers.

Those who hadn't been buried at sea now lay on the decks, gone from this world and left to rot.

And Jonah, having taken the helm, guided the ship along, singing shanties and sailing for dark waters.

Vindictive Waters

by Ali House

The attack was swift and merciless. By the time the crew noticed the *Jolly Roger*, it was too late. Pirates swarmed the ship—sharp blades in their hands and murder in their eyes. Soon the entire crew lay dead on the blood-soaked deck.

The unmanned ship was left adrift, with nobody to guide it. But as the moon ascended, the spirits of the dead began to rise.

It was rumoured that pirates felt no fear, but they'd always been the hunter, never the hunted. As the ghostly crew manned their stations, they swore never to rest until they'd tasted revenge.

On a Ship, a Black Freighter

by Joachim Heijndermans

We be a happy crew once. There was rum, spoils, and women. So many women, all who stopped struggling once the cutlass touched their necks.

We shouldn't have taken her. If we'd known what she'd truly been. Not a lass, but—

Now we sail. We sail on this demon of a ship. She claws at us as we hoist the sails. Teeth that rip our souls apart.

We sail on this ship, a black freighter. We raid, but there be no joy. Only the pain we inflict, tripled on ourselves.

Lord have mercy. But He can't see us no longer.

The Red Fleet

by R.A. Goli

The pirates spilled from the docks and into the village. They were after food, silk, and animal hides. Women, too.

Elizabeth ran back to her cottage, remembering the rough hands of the man who'd used her for his pleasure last time.

She released her familiars. By nightfall, a hundred rats invaded the ship and hid until the pirates set sail. Then they attacked.

These rats carried a disease new to these men. Soon their gums would bleed and teeth would fall out. Their bones would become brittle and pustules would burst from their skin.

The Red Fleet would never return.

Freeflint's Final Escape

by Chris Hewitt

"Hanging is too good for him," the Governor had declared. "Decency demanded justice and an example."

Forgoing the execution, they'd clapped Freeflint in irons and hung him naked from the dockside gibbet for all to witness.

"You shan't escape this time," promised the Governor, placing guards on watch.

Freeflint lasted an agonising week before succumbing to dehydration and the elements. Not that death prevented his last escape. The sun might have taken the Pirate Captain's skin and the seagulls his eyes, but his loyal crew claimed the rest, one pound of flesh at a time, as each paid their final respects.

The Pirate's Jewel

by Andrew Kurtz

Max listened as the freak show owner addressed the crowd. "In this coffin are the remains of the bloodthirsty pirate, Orange Beard, who removed the hearts of his victims."

Inside was a skeleton with a shredded black eye patch and a bright red jewel in its ribcage.

"The jewel is said to be cursed," the owner warned.

After the freak show closed, Max snuck back into the tent, but when he lifted the coffin lid, he emitted a bone-chilling scream.

When the owner opened the coffin during the next show, there was a human heart nestled next to the jewel.

The Harikikigaki Has the Answer

by Kelly Matsuura

A weak pulse, lethargy, and fainting spells—Dr Yamata knew his wife was infected by a yōkai parasite. But which one?

"We shouldn't have gone camping," he mumbled, searching for his copy of *The Harikikigaki*, an ancient acupuncture text.

Later, he found Chiho unconscious in their backyard. As he desperately tried CPR, a tiny red-and-white horse escaped Chiho's mouth with her final breath.

The doctor hadn't found the textbook, but the umakan was unmistakable.

With a soft whinny, it flew next door, where the neighbour was burning leaves.

Dr Yamata would be seeing Mr Enami at his clinic very soon.

Parachnoids

by Karen Bayly

"Parasitic arachnoids," declared the entomologist. "Deadly."

I'd laughed. "Pull the other one. I'll be okay."

Famous last words. There must be hundreds of the little bastards nestling in my flesh. I feel them eating, scratching, spreading, pushing upwards from within.

I can handle the legs growing out the edges of my nipples that look like wayward hairs. And the bristles all over my back and limbs aren't so bad.

But it's the eyes, man, the eyes. Popping up everywhere. Body, earlobes, eyelids, lips, even my penis. Damn. The tip of my dick has eight compound spider eyes.

Kill me. Please.

Chastened

by Patrick Winters

A blonde bombshell was walking Denny's way.

As she passed by with a flirtatious smile, his cheeks went red, and a lewd thought about her lips came crisp and clear to his mind.

An instant later, a wild flare of pain racked his body. The worst of the agony ignited in his nether regions, setting them afire. It was enough to bring tears.

As the sensation ceased, he heard that whisper in his head: The only desires you should think of are mine.

Denny, bowing to the thing inside him, moved along, head hung low, avoiding every woman he could.

We Are Family

by Nicole Little

I tried to stay calm.

But I could feel it moving.

My small cry of revulsion alerted him that I was awake. He approached from across the bunker and I cringed.

"How are you feeling?"

"Sick."

"It won't last forever." He sat on the bed, adjusted my restraints. "It will be worth it."

Tears stung my eyes. "Please. It will kill me."

He edged closer, lightly caressed my stomach.

It rippled in response.

I screamed.

"You should be honoured, dear Emily." All four insectoid eyes gleamed with satisfaction. "It's the dawn of a new world. And you will be Mother."

The Dancer

by Lyndsey Ellis-Holloway

It was the latest craze. All dancers were doing it.

How else did one stay thin enough to be on top?

Pills didn't work, diets were useless—what was the harm in cheating a little?

Lucy's flexibility had got her noticed.

The way her body moved and swayed with eerie grace. She stretched, twisted, and turned in ways other ballerinas could only *dream* of.

So thin. So beautiful. So talented.

Little did they know. Lucy was long gone.

The tapeworm egg she had swallowed and allowed to develop had taken over her entire body.

It had always wanted to dance.

Beauty Mark

by Chisto Healy

Lara had first seen it on her shoulder. She had been outdoors that day and wearing a tank top. She figured it was a sunspot, a new freckle, some might say a mole. Lara preferred beauty mark. It was cute.

Then it wasn't.

Lara's little brown spot grew and stretched. It became scaly and raised as it multiplied, now five thick lines reaching to a large brown base, like a dark hand gripping her back.

She thought it was some kind of infection or disease until she heard its voice inside her mind. It said, "Kill."

Crawl

by Sophie Wagner

"Please!" the hysterical mother shrieked. "You have to help her; she's going to die!"

"Mrs," the doctor replied. "We are doing everything we can. We've never seen anything like this before."

The girl who sat in front of them, once a healthy athlete, was now frail and almost transparent. Her hair was slicked with sweat from a fever that you could feel from halfway across the room. And worst of all, black lines traced up and down her veins.

Suddenly she began to convulse and fell to the floor. A dark shape appeared under her skin.

It began to crawl.

Soul Fungus

by Simon Clarke

Every day as darkness falls and the day's echoes falter to silence, my existence slips further away. Primordial spores now infect my mind, connecting to a past that isn't mine.

Complex toxins cling to every moist membrane, burning my guts as my soul slowly rots.

Soon I will forget the afternoon I dozed too long amongst ancient trees, waking covered with a fine layer of pale filaments, brushing them off too late.

Unearthly enzymes dissolve and digest my being, fusing with my DNA. Before long I will be gone. It will become me completely, ready to join with you all.

The Most Natural Thing on Earth

by Gemma Paul

It burns her insides, itching to get out.

She clutches desperately at her throat and gags loudly—a deep, hoarse sound erupts from her lungs as she struggles to breathe. She throws her head over the toilet basin, but nothing comes out.

She can feel it inside. Squirming around. Twisting and turning. Its heart beats steady inside, a stark contrast to her erratic one.

It's ready to come out. She can feel it.

No one ever told her it would be like this. It's natural they say. To her though, growing a baby, inside her womb is her worst nightmare.

The War Earth Won

by Gary Smith Jr.

The world is a better place. Years ago, people abused her, taking resources that could never be replaced, giving back pollution, hate, and violence.

The planet was the real winner in the war between the humans and parasites. She barely noticed the increase of death and destruction during the decades of war. The bodies of humans and parasites alike nourished her back to health soon after.

Earth now receives the attention she deserves, love and caring she is owed for her eons of giving. Yes, without people the world is a better place. The parasites that remain love her well.

In Control

by Constantine E. Kiousis

The man stood at the edge of the precipice, staring solemnly at the angry tide below, a bottle of scotch dangling from his fingers.

Even though it was asleep, he could still feel it, wrapped around his brain, squirming. All the shit it'd made him do as he'd watched helplessly, seldom allowing him control… But he'd used that time wisely. He'd learned it couldn't hold its liquor.

Breathing deep, he stepped off the ledge.

He sensed it waking as he plummeted, sensed its horror as it shrilled.

He closed his eyes, managing a defiant grin before crashing against the waves.

Under Your Skin

by Brandi Hicks

I skitter over skin, searching for the perfect spot. My host can't see me as I dig through her dermis, but soon enough she'll feel me. She's done nothing wrong; she just tastes oh-so-sweet and was in the wrong place when I caught her scent. I'm at her muscle now, the sinewy goodness quenches my hunger-lust momentarily.

It's time for the fun to begin.

My pincers snip away at tissue, I don't need it but I want it. I hear her now, my venom filling her, making her scream in agony. I call for my siblings. Let our plague begin.

Visceral

by Bernardo Villela

Malcolm awoke confused. Eyes stung from something acidic.

In pitch blackness he groped for his phone. Flashlight on.

A corrugated ceiling. No, *a tunnel.*

He touched the floor. Not rocky, covered in dark sludge and liquid. A muscular firmness and tissular feel. Fingerlike protuberances brushed against his hand. A noxious breeze blew.

Gaseous.

Sludge slid, knocked him about. Bumping his head into what felt like mucus, he recalled: a face fourfold his size, a gaping maw, being swallowed.

The giant thought he killed me.

Malcolm gnawed on its intestinal wall. His oxygen limited, he ate in hopes of freeing himself.

Bot Flies

by Lynne Phillips

Zacji didn't feel the bites, but as his body heated, his arm began to itch. Hundreds of tiny larvae wriggled in waves under his skin emerging through his pores, their heads taking a breath before disappearing and wriggling again. They moved like rivulets along his arm towards his shoulder.

Using the edge of his knife he frantically scraped his arm, removing his skin and the larvae, seeking relief.

Realising they had moved across his shoulders and down his left arm, squirming towards his wrist, emerging as bot flies, Zacji screamed in agony and collapsed, unable to bear the paralysing pain.

Twelve Drums

by Maxine Churchman

The drums sounded sweet. Jack said he would show me how he got those wonderful tones. An extractor fan whirred and clanked ineffectually against the putrid smell in the chilly workshop.

"I need one more, twelve drummers drumming and all that." He was obsessed with Christmas.

"Chemicals of the trade," he said, laughing at my streaming eyes.

He picked up a frame over which a skin was stretched so thinly it was almost see-through.

"See that mark? It's too identifiable." He ripped it from the frame and turned his dark eyes on me. "You don't have any birthmarks do you?"

The Madman's Song

by Darlene Holt

"On the twelfth night of Christmas, my killer gave to me:

> *twelve hours stalking,*
>
> *eleven haunting phone calls,*
>
> *ten severed fingers,*
>
> *nine pleas for mercy,*
>
> *eight ripped out teeth,*
>
> *seven fatal stab wounds,*
>
> *six organs bleeding,*
>
> *five chilling screams,*
>
> *four shattered ribs,*
>
> *three gasping breaths,*
>
> *two arms tied,*
>
> *and a corpse hanging in an elm tree."*

The madman's song whisks through the brisk December breeze. The Santa-clad monster grins, crimson suit vibrant against pallid skin like the blood-speckled snow below. He saunters away, still smiling, and the world darkens—my last morsel of life draining from my dangling, mangled body.

Ten Lords Tumbling

by Kimberly Rei

The mall was three storeys tall, with a spacious central opening and a gathering area at the bottom.

The first man to crash down landed as the relentlessly joyful Christmas carol sang "a partridge in a pear tree." We all stared in horror as verse after verse, another body fell. All men, each with a word attached to their chest.

Confusion scattered the screaming crowds. I saw him smile from above.

My truest love, he had claimed. I knew what the words would spell out: his response to my refusal.

"If you don't marry me, my heart shall surely break."

Nine Ladies Dancing

by Charlotte Langtree

They mesmerised him, nine beautiful women seducing him with every spin and flash of bare legs. He was the last man in the club but he didn't care; he had enough cash to keep them dancing. It was almost Christmas, his divorce was finalised, and he felt like celebrating.

"How much for even more fun?" he slurred.

The ladies smiled. When he spotted the glint of sharp teeth between their lips, he put it down to cheap vodka and expensive coke. As they gathered round, sinking their teeth into his veins, the pleasure stole his breath. They stole his life.

Under the Mistletoe

by Amber M. Simpson

Aaron held Mia in his arms, slow dancing across his candlelit living room to Bing Crosby's "White Christmas."

Her head rested on his shoulder, long hair cascading down his arm. His heartbeat raced from the nearness of her. Holding her like this was a dream come true.

With subtle deliberation, he swept her towards the doorway where the mistletoe hung, eager for the kiss he'd been longing for all night.

He lowered his head to hers, pressed his mouth to her cold, lifeless lips.

"Merry Christmas," he murmured against her neck, covered with the deep purple bruises he'd left there.

Seven Swans A-Swimming

by Ali House

Chloe awoke touching something wet. As the fog clouding her mind lifted, she realised that the floor she was lying on was covered with an inch of water.

The room was unfamiliar, as were the six terrified women trapped with her. Nobody could remember how they got there or knew how to get out.

Suddenly the water began to rise. Within seconds, it was almost waist high. They cried out for help, searching frantically for an escape.

Their abductor watched from another room. As the water reached shoulder height, a wicked smile crossed his face.

"You'd best start swimming, my little swans."

Up on the Rooftop

by Warren Benedetto

There was something on the roof.

The children huddled behind the couch, their tearful eyes glistening in the warm glow of the Christmas lights. The house shook with each heavy footfall thudding overhead. Plaster dust drifted from the ceiling like snow. A low growl echoed down the chimney, followed by the metallic scraping of a heavy blade.

"What was that?" Annie whispered, her voice trembling.

"I don't know," Joshua sobbed. "Do you?"

He directed the question at the fat man in the red suit cowering behind the couch next to them.

Santa shook his head, his eyes wide with fear.

Yule Dig It!

by Steven Holding

He loathed the season of goodwill, but festive choirs congregating upon his doorstep really got his goat.

Red-cheeked warblers, arriving unannounced, expecting pennies for their impromptu performance!

Dozing, jarring harmonies awoke him. "The Twelve Days of Christmas"! He grimaced, determined to ignore the lyrical list of gifts being delivered at his door.

It got worse with each verse, until line number five. Like a broken record, the same three words repeated.

Barging outside, he shuddered at the sight of pale strangers bearing presents.

Five gold rings on five severed fingers, held in the cold dead hands of five carol singers.

Carrion

by Rich Rurshell

On the fourth day of Christmas, my true love sent to me, four colly birds…

If true, then Mother Nature is my true love. I won't argue with that. I always loved nature.

I'm not sure why I stayed here. Leaving doesn't seem appropriate.

Not while I'm like this.

These carrion crows are the only living things to have paid me any attention. If I can still call this me. A lifeless corpse staring into the winter sky from this ditch.

Just days ago, I was eating turkey. Now the birds feast on me. Nature's way of redressing the balance.

Cookies for Santa Claws

by Chanelle Loftness

"You better not cry," the creature croons.

I lie on the kitchen table. The Christmas lights that bind me dig into my skin. They send colours dancing across the kitchen's walls and illuminate the creviced face of the sharp-toothed and horned creature standing over me.

"You better not pout." Its sharp talons cut another piece of my flesh.

Wide-eyed, I scream around the Christmas stocking in my mouth.

It places the flesh on the cookie sheet by the others, dusting them with cinnamon and sugar, before sliding the sheet into the oven.

It continues singing as it grabs another cookie sheet.

On the Feast of Stephen

by Jean Martin

Under the old king, it would have been the Feast of Stephen, the second day of Christmas.

But our new king took us back to the Old Gods and the old ways.

As he decreed, nine men and nine women were offered in sacrifice that morning, in the woods, near the spring that had been named for Saint Agnes.

The snow lay roundabout deep and crisp and scarlet. There was steam rising in the frosty air from the hot blood.

One small page, lying still on the ground, his dead eyes staring wide and empty at the grey winter sky.

Silenced Night

by Constantine E. Kiousis

Colourful lights twinkled around the Christmas tree as muffled screams filled the darkened living room, Marie gawking from a corner as the hulking man stuffed her terrified mother into a huge linen sack before fastening it shut.

Hoisting the bag over his shoulder, he glanced towards the girl, moonlight glinting off his jolly eyes as he winked at her, a toothy smile across his soot-smudged, white beard. Turning, he ambled to the fireplace, the bag's insides squirming, her parents' stifled protests fading as he went up the chimney.

She couldn't believe it.

Santa had gotten her letter!

No more bedtime!

YEAR TWO

PATREON

BLACK HARE PRESS

The Book of the Dead

by David Green

I found no record of the book being at the Miskatonic University, but it was there I discovered it, hidden away under lock and key. I knew before opening the safe what I would encounter inside. Bound in leather, its metal clasps opened with an inviting click. The *Kitab al-Azif,* in my hands at last.

My trembling fingers flipped the pages until a phrase caught my eye. Without thinking, I uttered its foreign words.

"Fahf shuggog ilyaa thee r'luhhor."

Ignorance has opened the way, and the fault is mine alone.

The *Old One's* return. I've doomed humanity to endless oblivion.

Raw Materials

by Tim Mendees

The door slammed behind him as he crashed into the wall, knocking a cheap print to the floor. He could still hear the strange chittering coming from his habitation unit. Mr Grant turned and sprinted as fast as he could in the direction of the stairs.

Each light fizzed and sparked as he passed under it. Whatever was stalking him wasn't far behind…creeping.

He took the stairs three at a time and was soon on the street. He ran as fast as he could. It wasn't fast enough. He didn't even make it to the end of the street...

Torn

by Stacey Jaine McIntosh

A girl is shackled to the concrete wall, cuffed with cold iron that bites into her skin.

Tears prick her eyes, but she refuses to cry.

"This is punishment for your crimes committed against the Winter Court."

In one fluid motion, the executioner tears her fragile wings from her shoulder blades, leaving her broken and bleeding. Rivulets of blood cascade down her back, turning her milky white skin crimson.

Keys jangle, bringing her out of her pain-fuelled daze, and back into the present—back to the smoke-filled nightclub with its live cover band.

"Ferelith!" the band's drummer Atticus shouts.

Whore

by Zoey Xolton

"Darling," croons the succubus.

"Yes, Lilith?"

"I'm bored."

"Bored? How can you be? There's more cock in Hell than anywhere else in the Verse."

Lilith crawls onto the Fallen angel's lap. "I crave an adventure," she pouts.

Lucifer sighs. "You're incorrigible."

"That's why you love me, my king," she whispers into his ear.

Lucifer's silver-blue eyes gleam as he smiles. "Just one of the many reasons," he concedes. "And you know that I can't say '*no*' to you."

Lilith bites her lip, pleading.

"As you wish," he grants. "How do you feel about putting your siren song to good use?"

Sex Type Thing

by S.O. Green

Lisa-Marie Kenyon was gone. The mousey-haired, doe-eyed, rabbit-toothed girl had transformed into a wolf.

Her name was Jezebel. Her band was Sin. So was her lifestyle.

They asked her the secret of their popularity. She said, "Me."

They asked her if she ever lip-synched. She said, "Only if I meet a girl I really like."

They asked her about the suicides. The bloody knives, the swinging ropes, the empty bleach bottles. She said, "It's beautiful, isn't it? To inspire so much passion."

"Isn't that kind of talk irresponsible?" they asked her.

"I believe in individual freewill," she said, "don't you?"

Jingle Bells

by Neen Cohen

She froze in the middle of aisle six.

It can't be.

But her ears hadn't deceived her—jingles Bells piped through the speakers. She dropped the half-filled basket of previously vital items and raced from the overexposed florescent lit store.

Her breathing was ragged as she closed the door behind her.

Her internal duality fighting.

She hated it. A smile oozed as she pushed off from the door. She loved it.

Reverently she placed the suit on her bed and striped away the laborious life.

She eagerly anticipated the headlines:

Murderous Santa returns, more severed heads left beneath Christmas trees.

The Drummer's Beat

by Brandi Hicks

Rat-a-tat-tat. Rat-a-tat-tat.

The drumbeat rang in her ears as she tried to wiggle out of her restraints. The blinking lights of the Christmas tree illuminated his face—off, on, off, on. Each time they flashed his menacing smile got closer; the drumbeat grew louder.

Rat-a-tat-tat. Rat-a-tat-tat.

She was hypnotized by the thumping rhythm. In a split-second, the baton went from his hand to her chest. She stared where it protruded, confused. He beckoned behind her, then a chorus of *rat-a-tat-tat* echoed through the room.

Blood seeped from her ears as the twelve drummers surrounded her, thirsty for her heart's beat.

The Good List

by Karen Bayly

The man on the slab stirred, felt the five sharpened steel rings digging into his neck, wrists, and ankles. Gold tinsel festooned each ring, adding insult to injury.

"Ho, ho, ho," chortled Santa. "Who's been a naughty boy?"

"Don't do this," begged the man.

Santa scratched his beard, deep in thought, shrugged, then flicked a switch. The rings hummed.

"Merry Christmas!"

The rings rotated, contracted, and sliced, spraying blood into the air.

The man's head dropped and rolled to rest against Santa's black boots, eyes wide, mouth still protesting.

The big guy grinned.

"You'd never make the good list, loser."

Squirmish

by Stefanie Elrick

"Who's your friend?" A mountain of leather and muscle grunts from under the archway.

"My date. It's her first time."

The doorman chuckles, low-bellied booms like subterranean detonations, then lollops to the side just enough to let the two girls squeeze past.

Inside it's clammy-hot; air so thick you could bite off chunks and chew it barely circulating between hot and unwashed bodies and four windowless brick walls. There's a sparsely stocked bar, complete with bored looking barmaid with a green Mohican and giant bullring through her septum, but no-one seems to be buying any drinks. At the centre of the room; a make-shift cage strung up around an improvised boxing ring, a square of grubby matts streaked with dubious stains and some strip lights, all flanked by mesh fences that slant precariously to the left.

The smaller of the two, the girl with jellyfish and octopi tattooed all over her anaemic looking skin, slips through the crowd like a minnow swimming upstream. Her guest, a bigger girl with dark skin the colour of fertile earth, gets tangled in the throng.

Vivica—or _FlyFishDish_ on her Freak4U profile—finds them seats close to the ropes, as close as can be without competing with the hyper-territorial regulars. These patrons, with their dough-white midriffs spilling out over elasticated sweatpants like melting candles, take up two or three ringside seats a-piece.

"So, you come here a lot?" Suneera asks as they finally sit down, flicking purple-green braids over her shoulder and draping her neon green puffa-jacket over the plastic seat.

"Sure, it's the only place nearby with all female contenders." Vivica smiles, tracing a grey-scale Japanese wave over her collarbones.

"Really?"

"Uhm. Not too sketchy is it?" The question's borne lightly, but hides a thinly veiled provocation.

Suneera smiles, revealing two chips of diamante bling adorning her canines, and tries to summon some quip about the filthier places she's been and/or seen. Before she does, somebody lumbers into her from behind and lands a sharp elbow into the back of her neck. Normally she'd stand up, drop a few ground-levelling word bombs and take the sucker down, but after weighing up the club's clientele she decides—*just this one time*—to pretend she hasn't noticed.

"What kind of fighting is it anyway? Mui Thai? Ju-Jitsu?" Suneera's dated a few wannabe UFC fighters. She's eager to prove she knows the lingo.

"A bit of everything." Vivica grins. "Girl-on-girl gets pretty wild."

And that's when the penny drops. Suneera's skim read some badly written E-zines all about this 'entertainment', and now the whole vibe of the Click-Clack Club makes sense. Still, for all her down-right tacky choice of first dates, weird little Vivica is definitely worth sticking around for.

A bell clangs and the lights cut out. An elliptical pool of dingy yellow appears in the centre of the ring. A huffing man in an oversized tux appears, clutching the mic to his chest like it's the last bottle of Jack Daniels left in the world.

"Ladies and not-so-Gentle-men, welcome to the Click-Clack Club. Prepare to see sights your Momma said would make you blind, that they've outlawed in sixteen different countries and that have been officially denounced by the Vatican! Watch our girls tough it out to become tonight's Deep One Queen and don't forget what day it is…Roulette Wednesday!! Which means open mat for all you punters!"

Vivica hollers loudly along with the rest of the crowd, slapping her cheek like an Indian Squaw and climbing up in her seat like an excitable child. She's only an outline in the shadows now, small as a prepubescent teenager, but Suneera feels the pheromones throb off her like gamma rays.

The hubbub grows quiet, signalling the first contender; there's no flamboyant high-fiving, no puffed-up entourage, not even any cocky entrance music, just an oddly reverent hush as a lone woman with pale lilac corn-rows walks unhurriedly towards the ring. Her skin's bone-pale, muscles well-sculpted, and her deltoids alone look like ribbed shoulder pads from the eighties. A noise begins. Suckling: compressed air forced in and out through many different sets of lips. Suneera shuffles uncomfortably in her seat and notices that Vivica is doing it too. The words spill out before she can check herself, "*What* the *hell*?"

Vivica giggles, bending down to shout in her ear, "She's called The Sucker."

A second fighter walks out, a short but pumped-up brunette with a low centre of gravity and quads the size of boulders. The noise changes, morphing into something more like the orf-ing of seals but minus the clapping.

"Let me guess," Suneera's snorts, "she balances shit on her nose?"

"That's The Skinner."

The ladies begin to stalk counterclockwise, flawlessly equidistant in a taught and glistening dance. The pale one towers like some Norwegian giantess whilst The Skinner's ass can't be more than a foot off the floor. They circle, slow and purposefully, to the middle before squaring up jaw to jaw. Both wear too-tight cut-off jeans and ludicrously skimpy bikinis.

"Ok Ladies." The man in the tux yells whilst triple bolting the only cage door from the outside. Turning to the crowd, he lifts his arms, goading them into a well-practised call-and-response. "You know the rules… THERE ARE NO RULES! *FIIIIIIIIIGHT!*"

As the bell clangs, Suneera glances reflexively back the way they came in. Someone tall must be stood right in front of the exit sign, either that or it's been switched off because now, like every other inch of this shitty little club, except for the light that's spotting the ring, there's nothing to see but darkness.

The fighters have resumed their predatory loop with wide, deliberate side-steps like mating crabs. The giantess hunches over, leaning forward, huge fingers opening and closing whilst the dark one shimmies and hops backwards and forwards, hissing and spitting indecipherable cusses on the floor. Both throw the odd leg kick or barely landing love tap, but there's no real intent or lethal force. Neither seemed to think it necessary to wrap their knuckles or wear gloves.

Abruptly the big one lunges, grabbing her opponent by her belt straps and lifting her clean off the ground. The smaller girl starts thrashing madly, screaming like a banshee in heat, and this is all in reaction to what Suneera can only interpret as the world's most excruciating wedgie. She sighs to herself; *this isn't hot in the slightest, just painfully, predictably cheap.*

The blonde starts turning, spinning the smaller airborne woman like a rag doll until (surprise, surprise!) her pants split, sending The Skinner hurtling against the fence. The hulk doesn't waste time for her rival to retaliate, instead she charges like a bull, slamming her forehead full-force into her sternum. Then, it appears as if she's motor-boating her— viciously ripping off The Skinner's bikini top with gold-grilled teeth.

Suneera unsuccessfully stifles a mocking groan.

"Seriously?"

Sliding a casual hand between her thighs, Vivica leans in and whispers in her ear, "Just wait."

The Skinner's started to fight back and has locked stocky legs around Albino-China's six-pack. She's also managed to somehow wriggle herself around to her back, and now clamps an arm around her neck in a pretty convincing looking choke hold. The blonde stands, lifting them both off the floor, as Latino-Queen screams like a pre-menstrual harpy, and of course, somehow in the tussle, her bikini's also come undone, unleashing two more silicone mammeries into the fray. Next, The Skinner arches and flips under, curling like an eel between the giantess' legs.

Suneera's less impressed by their gymnastic choreography than the inquisitive fingertips brazenly grazing her panties in the dark. From that moment on her attention's severely divided, and she's only vaguely aware when the crowd begins cheering 'cos The Skinner's shorts are torn off in revenge.

A rush of heat as Suneera closes her eyes, grunting delicately, glad to lean into nuzzle Vivica's shadowy neck. A series of ooh's and aaah's are all she hears as she buries her face into her soon-to-be lover's skin. Vivica's neck is lean, pungent, and Suneera nips her playfully with her teeth.

There's a blood-curdling war-cry before the crowd resumes their baritone orfs. Startled, Suneera glances back to the ring, squinting through the murk at the scene in front of her. The tall blonde is now suddenly completely bald, and the crowd is screeching and roaring. Straddling the bigger girl from behind now, The Skinner's twisted her elbow into an excruciating arm lock. She keeps on the pressure whilst brandishing a corn-row wig in the air above the women pinned flat on her belly. The thing she holds is wet and its dripping. The Sucker's scalp glistens fresh wound raw red.

"Did you just…?"

Vivica grabs Suneera's chin and kisses her full on the mouth, forefingers pushing roughly inside. *Prosthetics, surely? It's all choreographed anyways, isn't it?* An expert tongue introduces itself to her tonsils.

Suneera can't dwell as Vivica devours her tongue and her lips sloppily before dramatically pulling away. Then, jerking Suneera's head roughly back towards the ring, Vivica's voice is rasping yet firm, "You don't want to miss this, Babe. Trust me."

The Skinner's started to rip pale strips of skin off

the other woman's back and blood splatters everywhere like a Jackson Pollock. The woman being peeled is buckling and moaning, caught between pain and pertinacious stimulation. There's a crack as her shoulder pops loose from its socket then twists at some horrifically irregular angle. Her blood's made everything slippery-smooth, so now the Skinner's lost her main advantage. But her broken arm is somehow reconfiguring itself, wasting no time in softening into something boneless and inhumanly limber. With a SLAPthis new appendage wraps itself around the other woman's neck, then tightens like a whip around her throat.

"That can't be real!" Suneera gasps, lapped by synchronous waves of arousal and confusion. Vivica responds by sticking a wet tongue in her ear.

Suneera's as dumbstruck as she is dripping-wet, and the scene before her is only getting weirder. The Skinner, apparently unfazed by asphyxiation, is digging her fingers inside the one-pack of her own stomach. With a jerk and a rip, she exposes the red-black muscles of her abdomen, taut and wetly crimson for all to see. Then, oblivious to pain and the threat of mortality, she yanks at those muscles 'til all that's left is a cat-flap sized opening in her gut.

Compliantly, some quivering mass squeezes through and flops out, leaving The Skinner's human form completely flaccid. The crowd has gone wild, barking and stomping their support, whilst Vivica fingers increase the rhythm of their friction.

"This isn't… I don't…" Suneera manages to blurt out, yet somehow is still unable to pull her eyes away. The jelly-thing shimmy-slides out from the walls of its human shell — now a liberated mound of shape-shifting goo. The giantess stands up, and with her human arm, methodically snaps her own neck before lapping a circuit of the cage, head swinging left to right like a hypnotist's pendulum. Out of her mouth, new limbs are wriggling free, thrashing lengths squirming out from the too-small hollow of her throat. They're suckered, dripping, writhing things that could extend to twelve or maybe even twenty feet at full length. Then, her human body is shucked off completely and abandoned in a crumpled pile on the canvas.

Now, two lumps of gambolling un-flesh frolic with careless abandon inside the fence which seems too full of holes to hold either inside. The Sucker's a jumble of cephalopod trails. The Skinner's a mound of sentient slime.

Suneera gasps, speechless and panting, as Vivica

pumps her swelling folds. Her insides are tightening and retracting at whim. Her pelvic floor clenched as tightly as her jaw.

The contenders—now irreversibly mutated—seem no less keen to compete. They charge, or rather spill, towards each other in a rush of liquid enthusiasm. The crowd has switched gears and are manically howling their support with sounds no human vocal cords could ever create: it sounds like the glugging of plugholes or a mad congregation choking on their tongues.

The room's stink has trebled into something like stagnant pond water and unseen horrors slap and slither in its corners. Something like panic rises from the pit of Suneera's stomach; a bubble of pressure ascending through her oesophagus, desperate to birth itself as a scream. With it something more ancient and cogent; a marrow-deep instinct to unstiffen and mutate. She doesn't have to look to know that Vivica has already obeyed it, and that the hand between her legs no longer has bones.

The next thing she hears is Vivica murmuring with a voice like the breaking of tides gasping, breathless, "So how's about it, Babe. You wanna try?"

BLACK HARE PRESS

Independence Days

by Fulvio Gatti

It all began when my left lung asked for independence.

She did it in a soft voice that I could hear in my head—a voice that, at first, I could not identify.

"You've been having breathing issues," she explained. "Well, that's me. I'm very tired, maybe even depressed."

Startled, I let her continue.

"It's all dark in here, you know. I've been working for you all these years. We were a great team, and it's something I'll never forget. But now I need more space," she said.

I smiled fondly, even though I had nobody to look at. "I understand," I replied. "Do you think maybe I should take longer breaths, so my chest stays bigger for a longer time?"

"That would be very nice of you. But, Silvio, my dear, I was thinking about something else."

"What can I do for you? Please, tell me!"

"Well, I was wondering if you could be so kind as to let me go."

"Let you go?"

"I'll leave during the night and you will feel no pain at all."

"But…how is it possible?"

"Just tell me you're all right with that, first."

"But…how will I breathe?"

"I spoke to my brother. He can do all the work by himself."

"Your brother?"

"Your right lung."

"Oh, I see."

"What do you think? May I go?"

I was so astonished I didn't know what to answer. But she was so cute, and in fact I could still live with a single lung in my body. As long as she could really leave my body by herself—I thought it very unlikely.

"All right, do what you wish."

I heard the voice bursting into a sudden joy. "Thank you, thank you so much! I knew you'd agree, I knew you would to that for me."

I nodded to myself and went to sleep.

***

The morning after, the breathing problem was gone, and I found a big scar, already healed, on the left side of my waist. I remembered the talk to my left lung—I had actually archived it as an alcohol hallucination—and wondered if it was possible that she had really left.

I booked an X-ray exam, and one week later, I got the answer. My left lung had left. I wished her good luck in my mind and I thought I heard a happy and distant "Thank you".

I got back to my life until, a month later, a masculine dark voice started talking to me. He identified himself as my right kidney.

"The Council of Organs has been talking a lot about how generous you were, by setting your left lung free," he said. "If you're in good health now, it's thanks to the great mood we are in."

Still, it seemed my right kidney had something to complain about. "I'm getting old and I can't do my job anymore, not as well as I once did. I lack motivation and passion. I should probably retire."

I flinched.

"So you're telling me you'd like to…stop doing your job?" I asked kindly, curious about what the farewell of the left lung had brought into my own body.

"Well, staying here without doing anything would be very boring. I was actually thinking of moving."

"You want to go away?"

"Yes, that was the idea. Of course, if you don't mind. My sister..."

"The left kidney?"

"Oh, you know her!"

"We have a long-time relationship. As I do with every one of you in there."

I heard him laughing loud.

"You're a great guy, Silvio. I will miss this when I'm gone. But let's not be sentimental. My sister can handle the job, so if you have nothing against it, I will leave tonight."

"Sure, why not?" I replied without thinking much. I could survive with only one kidney, anyway.

My right kidney thanked me many times.

The morning after, he was gone, and I had a brand new scar.

***

Just a few days later, I felt a sudden aching in my penis as I was peeing. I had to sit down on the toilet because of the pain.

"Hello there!"

It was a girl.

"Shouldn't you be a guy?" I wondered.

"After all these years together, you're still so unfair to me," she said, barely hiding the bitterness.

"Like it was a matter of gender in any way!"

"No, but..."

"It's horrible down here, I'm always in the middle of dirty things."

"Come on, sometimes it's quite pleasant," I joked.

She groaned. "Not much, recently. And to be very honest, you haven't been very good at choosing your sex partners."

"That's your opinion, of course."

"Oh, yeah! When someone agrees with you, it's truth. When someone disagrees, it's just one's opinion. I'm very sick of this!"

"I'm sorry."

"No excuses, Silvio, I'm the one who does all the awful things here, and it's not possible you set free the first, cheerful lung that asks you permission to go, and meanwhile I'm still down here doing my job. You've always mistreated me, but now I'm fed up!"

I paused, worried about where the conversation may lead. "Is there something I can do to improve your conditions, my dear?" I asked in the sweetest tone I could muster.

"Of course you can. Let me go!"

"But it's not like the lungs or the kidneys. I still

have one of each of those. You are a one and only."

"You know that, please don't make things worse!"

"I mean, I cannot live without you."

"Only now, in the end, you understand my importance, huh? No way. Your words will not change my mind. I'm out tonight."

I was on the brink of pure horror.

"Please, think about it. How could I ever have sex if you go away?"

"Well, I haven't done that part of the job, the 'at attention' thing, in a long time. You can live without it, trust me. No woman will complain."

"But I need you for urinating!"

"I will leave a catheter behind, of course."

She didn't want to listen to reason, and the next morning I had lost my penis. But yes, there was a catheter there and peeing operations, even if a bit uncomfortable at first, could be still accomplished.

***

My health kept being excellent, but I spent my next days worried at the idea of hearing another organ asking for independence. All that stuff started to keep me up at night.

One night my heart started talking.

"Oh, Silvio, I love you so much that I could never

leave you," she said.

I exhaled.

"Of course, you and me know I'm the one who convinced you to let the lung, the kidney and the penis go," she said.

"I don't remember talking to you," I pointed out.

"But of course, it was a decision coming from your heart."

I groaned.

"Let's not get mushy, now. I wanted to tell you that the Council of Organs has been working hard, lately. I spoke on your behalf, explaining that the independence was not something that could be done without rules."

"Really?"

"Large intestine and small intestine are very good guys, you know?" my heart said.

"I guess so."

"Working together, they were able to work out the perfect order in which the organs can leave your body without harming you."

"Oh, yeah, that's fantastic," I commented without even trying to fake happiness.

"I know how you feel, my dear. But it's something that must be done for the safety of everybody."

"Well, the only one that risks his life, here, is me..."

"Silvio, come on! You're just a bit shocked. I miss the guys too. The penis, especially, was a great girl. A tight gal, on her good days."

"Was that a joke?"

"No, of course not. I'm very sorry if you even thought it was."

"All right, it's over. No more independence to anybody, here." I uttered the words, expecting to sound as harsh as possible.

"If you put it that way, there's not much to talk about. It was an act of kindness. You can't stop us."

***

The next few days I woke up without, in order, an eye, the right hand, the liver, both ears—I could still hear, they explained, since the only part that was gone were the auricles—the whole left leg from the hip to the foot, the teeth.

I started to use a crutch to move and carefully avoided the mirror, because I became angry as hell every single time something reminded me of the crippled man I had become because of that bunch of selfish jerks.

"Hello, Silvio!"

"What now?"

The large intestine was a good guy, I remembered. Still, not a good reason to bother me.

"Are you pissed?" he asked.

"I am, but go on," I replied. "Make my day."

"Maybe it's not the good time..."

"It never is. Tell me. What do you want?"

"Just wondering if you are all right," he said in a cautious voice. "It all feels a bit unbalanced in here— like you've been extremely nervous all day. Have you tried yoga?"

I growled, covering him with every insult I could think of.

***

During the night, I slipped out of my skull.

My body stopped living that very moment, and I felt relieved and avenged at the same time.

I'm a smart, tidy and charming brain in a test tube now. I take my time, think a lot, but the best part is that I don't have to share anything with anyone now.

They are all gone for good.

I have no news about those who had left when my body was alive. But certainly, those who were still in there the night I broke out of my skull are now food for worms—that's a nice thought.

I have to admit that sometimes, at night, I feel a bit lonely. But then I remember what a crazy time it was when all my organs were clamouring for independence.

Being whole wasn't such a big deal.

Total Immersion

by David Green

"Prepare for total immersion," the lush, female voice purrs. Excitement bubbles in my chest. I bite my lip as I stare into complete darkness, the weight of the virtual reality headset almost forgotten.

I received the invitation in an email from something called The Collective. Most of the time, I'd have ignored it, but the subject line hooked me.

Dale. Experience the thrilling life you desire. Total Immersion: unlock your fantasy with a Virtual Reality game like no other.

The possibilities unfurled in my mind. They started small; sex with Scarlett Johansson, then a night with the 1983 Swedish national volleyball team.

No, a weekend.

How's about telling my dad what I've always wanted to tell him? Belittle him. Make him feel as small as he did to me. Punch my boss.

Better yet, *kill* the fucker.

I arrived at the bottom of the email. My finger hovered over the icon to sign-up.

Why not do all those things? I thought. And more.

Anything! I glanced at my VR headset gathering dust beneath my gaming rig.

"What have I got to lose?" I muttered.

Then, I waited.

The anticipation of diving into Total Immersion consumed me. Every ping from my cell phone had me diving for it. I tossed it aside with frustration more than once when it didn't deliver what I craved.

Weeks passed at a glacial pace and I gave up hope.

"Spam mail," I said, refreshing my emails one long afternoon. "Some scammers got all my info."

The sign-up hadn't asked for any bank details, or else I wouldn't have agreed. Just my full name, age, gender and alternative email.

I'd checked that account more than once, too.

Today, I got out of the shower and checked my cell phone. An email waited for me.

'Welcome to Total Immersion.'

I launched myself at my gaming rig, damp and naked. My fingers trembled as I opened the email and clicked the download link. I grabbed my VR headset, blew away the dust, and fired it up.

The darkness brightens. I hear the slow, gentle slosh of waves. I'm sitting on a beach. White sands and blue skies above. It's clearer than reality.

"Dale?"

I turn my gaze from the sky.

Scarlett Johansson sits in front of me. Naked.

"Let me take control, Dale."

She leans forward. I can see the vein in her perfect neck pulse. Scarlett lifts her hands and places them against my temples.

Pain. Searing agony shoots from my head. My vision turns red. I raise my hands to fight her off, but she pushes me to the ground and pins my forearms with her knees.

"Thank you for playing," she whispers. "Your essence makes The Collective grow."

I feel hot liquid gush from my ears, my eyes, nose and mouth. Glancing down, I see a watery grey fluid mixed with the blood streaming onto my chest.

"Goodbye, Dale," Scarlett says.

My vision fades to black as Scarlett Johansson's perfect, beautiful face smiles at me.

BLACK HARE PRESS

Acknowledgements

When we embarked on our Black Hare Press journey back in late 2018, we never envisioned the huge support we'd get from the writing community. We have been truly humbled by the number of submissions we've received.

So, thank you to everyone who crafted tales just for us—from the tiny tales in our Dark Drabbles series to these speculative stories in this 500 Fiction series—we thank you from the bottom of our hearts.

To our families and friends, collaborators, random strangers who took pity on us, and everyone who has helped us on the way: we couldn't have done it without you.

Special thanks to our Patreon supporters, especially Brandi Hicks, James Aitchison and Jonathan Stiffy. Take a look at the Patreon-only content and merch here—patreon.com/blackharepress—and consider helping us get to the next stage.

And to you, our discerning reader, we and these talented writers did it all for you. We hope you enjoyed these tales, and if you did, don't forget to leave a review.

Love & kisses, Ben & Dean

www.blackharepress.com

BLACK HARE PRESS